Y0-BXV-295

BY NORMAN KOTKER

FICTION

Billy in Love

Learning About God

Miss Rhode Island

Herzl the King

HISTORY

New England Past

*Massachusetts:
A Pictorial History*

The Earthly Jerusalem

*The Holy Land in the
Time of Jesus*

Norman Kotker

Billy in Love

𝒵

ZOLAND BOOKS

Cambridge, Massachusetts

First Edition published in 1996 by
Zoland Books, Inc.
384 Huron Avenue
Cambridge, Massachusetts 02138

Copyright © 1996 by Zane H. Kotker

PUBLISHERS NOTE
This book is a work of fiction. Names, characters, places,
and incidents are either the product of the author's
imagination or are used fictitiously. Any resemblance to
actual events or persons, living or dead,
is entirely coincidental.

FIRST EDITION

Cover illustration by Karen Watson

Woody Herman photograph © Herb Snitzer

Book design by Boskydell Studio

Printed in the United States of America

02 01 00 99 98 97 96   8 7 6 5 4 3 2

This book is printed on acid-free paper, and its binding
materials have been chosen for strength and durability.

Library of Congress Cataloging-in-Publication Data
Kotker, Norman.
Billy in love / Norman Kotker. — 1st ed.
p.   cm.
ISBN 0-944072-68-2 (alk. paper)
I. Title.
PS3561.O844B55 1996   96-16503
813'.54 — dc20   CIP

for CYNTHIA

[1]

Joyce and Billy

THIS TIME I'm going to get married in white.

When I got married the first time, we went to City Hall on our lunch hour and had the ceremony performed by a judge. I never would have done it that way except for the fact that my father wouldn't pay for a wedding. "Anybody but Monroe," he said. "Otherwise I'd be happy to." Just because he didn't approve of certain of Monroe's associates. "What kind of wedding would it be if you have to tell the guests to park their guns at the door?" That's what he said to me. I was very hurt. Just because Monroe had to know a few people like that because of business, it didn't mean I was marrying them. Monroe had nothing to do with guns. All the years we were married, I never heard a thing about guns. So we went to City Hall. We had two taxi drivers for bridesmaids. The meters were ticking all the way through the ceremony. Everyone thought it was a scream, except for my mother and father and my in-laws.

That marriage worked out fine: thirty-seven years. This one will too. They used to say about Monroe: He's one in a million. Even my father came round to saying it eventually. Well, Billy's one in a million too. I haven't once made a mistake and called him Monroe, but once he called me Alice in the middle of the night. So what. He's thoughtful, he's sweet, he's always full of compliments, which I don't really need; I've had my share.

I went over to Palm Beach and bought a white crepe swirl skirt, $239. Thank God they're showing white now. I don't dare say what the blouse cost — if Billy knew, he'd have a heart attack — but I will say this: It cost even more than the skirt, and it was worth it, white satin and old-fashioned looking, with a high collar. My figure's not perfect, but it still looks good. I wish I could say the same for my neck.

I'm superstitious. Last time, I wore a skirt and a blouse too, powder blue, something you could wear to the office, not exactly powder, a little darker, more like baby blue. When the third baby turned out to be another boy, Monroe said, "Maybe you should have worn something pink the day we got married."

They've stopped using the name Joyce. I was the first Joyce around. Then there were quite a few Joyces. Then there weren't any Joyces anymore. When I was about fifteen, that's when the last baby named Joyce was born. I'd give my eyeteeth to see a new baby named Joyce. Maybe not my eyeteeth. I'd give a hundred dollars.

Billy wears partial dentures unfortunately. Upper left side. But he's got a wonderful head of hair.

SHE IS REALLY SOMETHING, let me tell you. You'd never guess her age. For that matter, from the way I'm acting, you'd never guess mine either. I feel like a twenty-year-old, so help me God. I don't think I ever had such a good time. Who would have thought old people could ever have so much on the ball? Sixty-nine. So that's what they've been talking about all these years. Sixty-nine. What an age! There I was up at the Entertainment Center, leading a pickup band — I volunteered, only golden oldies, thank God for that; I hope I never have to do any rock and roll again — and I spotted her dancing with some old guy, not her husband. I could tell that right away. The minute I saw her she just knocked me out. Please let me explain. How can I complain? She's the one I yearn for. She's the one I burn for. So much more beautiful than all the rest. I've seen thousands of them dancing. They don't measure up to half of her, I'm not talking measurements, but there too, like I said: How can I complain? She measures up perfect.

If there's one thing I've seen a lot of it's women dancing. What a nice sight. They used to come up to the bandstand while I was standing there holding the clarinet and they'd check out the signboard — Billy Symmes and His

Paper Moons — and they already had a few drinks in them, so they'd start squealing: "Billy Symmes! Didn't you do the Freeman affair?" Freeman or Newman or Goodman or whatever. I always said yes because I had nothing to lose and it's hard to remember every single affair. They're standing there in front of the bandstand and they start in swaying. They're shuffling. They swing. They swivel. They're all flushed and you can see their boobies moving around because they're breathing hard from all that exercise. God knows where their husbands are. Dancing with some tootsie from the other side of the family, maybe a sister-in-law, maybe a cousin who he's been eyeing for twenty years; and these babes start in on me, they get themselves fixed at me and they start jiggling away. If I was backup and not the one out front with the clarinet, the one calling out "Hully Gully" at them, making them swivel around, they wouldn't look at me twice. But I've got a good voice. That gets them. I'm tall and that gets them too. Once, one of them — she was wearing practically nothing on top. Nothing! — she comes up and asks me could she "blow a few licks on that clarinet of yours." Those exact words. "Now or later?" I said to her, "Now or later or both?" She winks at me and calls me fresh. Me! So I handed her the clarinet and she starts blowing on it like a pro.

Even so, Joyce is way superior. In public, a lady. In private. Well, that's private. Joyce. She's the one I burn for. Joyce. Joyce. Joyce. Joyce. Joyce.

I'm in demand. There's widows all over the place. Go down to the swimming pool: widows. Even in the wood-working shop: widows. Younger widows too. Maybe they're divorcées. But I don't want that. They're nothing but a bunch of hard luck stories. Their alimony stops, their kids are always in some kind of trouble. Even when I work out at the gym, there are widows hanging around outside the door. You can't escape them. Not that I want to. Walking down the aisle. Walking down the aisle. We will come rejoicing walking down the aisle. There's no reason to look around elsewhere once you get hooked up with Joyce. Joyce. How can I complain? Joyce. I could eat her up.

I'M GIDDY. He went out and bought me an engagement ring. An engagement ring, like kids, only not a diamond. A diamond is the last thing I need. So cute. Last week I said to him, "Don't think of buying me a ring, I've got enough rings." It's true. Every year when we went on our cruise Monroe would buy his Chivas Regal and I'd buy a ring. I got one in Curaçao, a big, square-cut emerald. Not just a cocktail ring either — a real emerald ring. I always wanted an emerald ring. We even went the very last year. I didn't want to go, but Monroe wanted to go, so there-fore we went. Those last three or four years with Monroe were no picnic when he would wake up in the middle of the night and have trouble catching his breath; and this was wrong and that was wrong and nothing worked right: heartbreaking.

"Buy me a flower instead," I told Billy. "A rose. No ring is as beautiful as a flower." It's true. Nature's jewels, that's what flowers are. So he went out and yesterday he came back with a rose in his hand and he handed it to me and I kissed him, a nice long kiss, thank you. And then all of a sudden he was standing behind my back, very close in, and both his arms were around me squeezing — I just love it when he does that — and he had something in his hand and then he spins me around and tells me to shut my eyes and so I shut my eyes and he covered them up with his hand and then he put a little box in my hand and there it was: a topaz ring. A topaz! At first I couldn't believe it.

Roy, joyce's oldest son, came down to check on the prenuptial. I can't say I blame him. There's a lot there, and by rights it should stay with her kids and not end up with me if she should — God forbid — happen to pop off before I do. I didn't dare ask Joyce if Roy's what Monroe looked like, with his bottom lip hanging down. Not handsome.

Roy looked over the agreement, and when he saw the

list of my cheesy CDs compared with her hundred-thousand-dollar Ginnie Maes, twelve and a half percent, he started tapping his finger against his bottom lip. But then he spotted my building. All he can see is the address, Commonwealth Avenue. There's no way he can tell how big the building is, how many apartments — only twenty-eight. There's no way he can tell how the furnace guzzles No. 2 oil either. But he smiled and he didn't look so worried anymore. Still, the idea of using only a Florida lawyer made him nervous. "You don't mind," he said to his mother, "let me shoot it up to Leon in New York."

Leon is a lawyer connected with their business, somebody's brother-in-law. The business is getting bigger. "My boys are doing wonderfully," Joyce told me one night, after, when we were just lying in bed talking. "They're outdoing their father."

The first night Roy came down, Joyce picks up my coffee cup — Sanka actually, coffee after dinner keeps me up — and starts walking into the kitchen. "Chat." She points out to the terrace. "I'll let you get to know each other." So we went outside to sit on the balcony.

It was getting dark, but there were still golfers down there. "They don't stop. They're fanatics," I told Roy. "They go on and on and they keep on going until they can't see to hit the ball anymore." But Roy didn't want to make conversation about the golfers. It was business, business for him. "How's music?" he says. "Music is jumping. I can tell that from my kids." Before I can answer, Roy starts bad-mouthing the fur business. "Fur is almost dead. We're getting out of fur," he tells me. They're moving into leather and suede, they're importing from Spain and China, only coats and jackets, big-ticket items. They set up a factory in Morocco. There's plenty to worry about in Morocco. "But if we get bounced out of there tomorrow, we still made back our investment already, and then some."

While Roy's in Florida checking out the prenuptial, his brother Danny's in Hungary, checking out leather. It made me itchy hearing about fur coats while I'm sitting there underneath the sheltering palms. But maybe it was talking to Roy that made me feel itchy.

NEW YORK IS WHERE MY MONEY — I ought to say Monroe's money — is going to end up, so Roy is right: we ought to work through a New York lawyer. Roy's got a good head for business. He inherited that from Monroe. When it was just Monroe running things, it was Monroe Tarlow Furs. Then it became Tarlow Fur and Leather. Plus Monette Furs. Now that the boys have taken over, it's Roydan Imports too. I only wish it was Royrobdan Imports, but Robert never wanted to go in with Monroe. He hated the idea, I don't know why. The other boys didn't mind, they were always there at the place, hanging around on Saturdays. Roy even learned how to be a cutter. Give him a pattern and a pile of skins and he can cut out a fur coat. He tacks it down and everything. He's really talented. But Robert wanted none of it, so now he's in with his father-in-law. Discount major appliances, a very tough business, lots of competition there. "Don't you just love Roy?" I said to Billy. "Isn't he a darling? Everybody thinks very highly of Roy. He's always doing things for other people."

"A nice kid." That's all Billy said. "Really nice."

He wasn't sounding very enthusiastic.

"Didn't you enjoy talking to him?" I asked him.

"Sure, sure. Really wonderful. An exceptional kid." Billy was giving me a little song and dance. A real musician. I could tell. So I changed the subject. I'm no fool. Billy and Roy don't have to be in love with each other. Billy and I do.

WHY SHOULD I TELL JOYCE that her kid kept quizzing me so much about Commonwealth Avenue that I finally got fed up and told him to check out the Assessor's Office in the City of Boston if he really needed to find out? "City Hall, Government Center, Boston, Mass.," I told him and then, sarcastic, "I don't know the zip." What am I going to tell Joyce: Roy has his eye out for the money? She knows that.

Roy comes back at me cool as a cucumber. "My secretary can find out the zip for me." Crisp as a cucumber too. "That's what she gets paid for."

"Are you really going to check it?" I couldn't believe what I was hearing.

"Just covering all the bases." He pushes his head forward and gives me this little wise-ass smile. That's how they operate in New York. They play tough. That's how Monroe made all his money. I heard it one day in the steam room from a guy who knew him in New York. It turns out Monroe wasn't just in the fur business. He was a loan shark too. Factoring they call it. He gave money to people the banks wouldn't touch because they were bad risks. High rates. And then if the risks didn't pay up, the collecting job got turned over to one of Monroe's buddies. Not a pretty business.

That was Monroe. That's where Roy was coming from. So what am I going to do? Tell Roy: Shove it. I'm going to marry his mother. That makes me almost like his father. I can't say: Mind your own beeswax. It's only the second time I ever even met the kid. I didn't want Joyce to catch on to how our conversation was going. All she could see was that we were smiling when she walked out onto the balcony where we were getting to know each other, like she wanted us to.

Let him check the Assessor's Office if that's what he wants to do. What do I care? I'm not going to let him know the mortgage is all paid off. It's none of his business. I've been advised that the smart thing to do is take out another mortgage on the building and put the money into treasury notes, but I don't want to go in that direction. It would have hurt Alice. Every month she used to tell me how much the mortgage had gone down by, and she worked out the day and date when it would all be paid off. She had this perpetual calendar in a leather frame that she picked up on sale somewhere. The date worked out to be on a Tuesday. Too bad she never lived to see the day. Sometimes on Tuesdays I think about it.

THE SECOND NIGHT ROY WAS HERE, he went back to his motel — he insisted on staying at a motel in Pompano. "You'll want your privacy," he said to me. I don't care about my privacy. My greatest pleasure is having my children near me. Well, maybe not my greatest, but one of my greatest. Maybe it's Roy who needs the privacy. I hope not. I hope he isn't running around. That isn't something he learned from his father; that wasn't Monroe's way. Usually it wasn't anyway. Once or twice, maybe. But after Roy explained that he wanted the motel so he could get in some ocean swimming, I didn't feel so bothered. He loves the ocean. The kids too; every summer they go out to Westhampton. Anyway, after Roy left and Billy left with him, I was in the bathroom washing my face and I heard a noise at the kitchen window, sort of scratching and tapping, terrifying. My door has a double lock and I had locked it so I wasn't too scared, but still you hear stories. So I went and looked out the kitchen window — I have the kind of glass where you can look out and they can't look in — and it was Billy!

I was furious. He had actually frightened me. I almost didn't open the door. But when I did open up for him, he was very sweet. He apologized and then he explained what happened. He had gone down and walked Roy to his car and then instead of going back home, he couldn't help it, he had to see me, he needed to be with me. So instead of even going home to telephone like he does sometimes and then asking me if he could come over, he just came. He had to, no question about it, he couldn't stand it, he couldn't wait. And then he got down on his knees in front of me and he started singing me a song: "I Can't Give You Anything But Love, Baby." And then he sat down next to me on the sofa and he started to hug me and kiss me; and then, need I say more?

That's Billy. He's a very unusual man. Right before Roy left, he said to me: "He's different from us, you know what I mean." I kind of knew what Roy meant. Billy is different. He hasn't had some of the advantages that come from having a little extra money. But I didn't want to say anything like that, so I asked Roy, "No, what do you mean? How is Billy different?"

Roy said: "Would I interfere?"

It's true. He'd better not interfere. I'd hate it if anybody interfered in what's my business, Billy's and mine, nobody else's. Billy's daughter-in-law is coming next month, Margery, I'm looking forward to meeting her. I really am. She does real estate. His son's a doctor and she sells real estate. That's just lovely.

"Let's go shopping," Joyce says to me the day after Roy goes back to New York. It's the hottest day of the year. The thermometer on the TV registers a hundred degrees, not a thermometer exactly, just a number. A hundred degrees, that's what it says. "It's too hot to go shopping," I tell her. "It's never too hot to go shopping." That's what she answers. "Never. Besides, the mall's air-conditioned. So is the car. Don't be like a sugar baby afraid to go out in the rain in case you might melt."

They love to go shopping here. That's what they do, they shop and shop trying to hold off the inevitable. They just move in and fix up their condos as fancy as they can and a month later they're out at the malls looking to buy a new chandelier.

Joyce goes to the closet and gets out her sweater and tries to hand it to me. "Can you carry this for me?" I tell her she's crazy. So she says something nobody can challenge. It's true, no fighting it: "It could be five hundred degrees out but the mall's still going to be cold." And she tosses the sweater toward me, underhand.

I don't want to go shopping. Shopping's the last thing I want to do. Is this going to be our first lovers' quarrel? Playfully like, I toss the sweater back at her, underhand too, right at her skirt. Bingo! Target — There's a happy land somewhere. But she puts her hand out and catches it before it hits target — you have to hand it to Joyce, she's got quick reflexes. Pop! Just like that sometimes — and she grins at me and throws the sweater back, fast. "Careful now," she says to me. "This sweater cost me eighty-five dollars."

I start inspecting the sweater. It's knitted out of some nylon kind of material, so it's got little holes all over it — drafts can come through — but it's got little pearls around the collar. I smell it — perfume. I run my lips over it. I start kissing it under the arms. You can tell which side is front because that's where the buttons are. I kiss the boobs, first one, then the other. Joyce is watching me, she's grinning, she's blushing. "Let's go," I say, and I wink at her. She's not sure what I mean. It's still morning, not yet time for a matinee. We just did it the night before. "Where do you want to go first? Jordan Marsh?" I like it that they have a Jordan Marsh in Florida. "Yes," she says. "Jordan Marsh." Jordan Marsh started in Boston so it makes me feel at home.

I ASKED BILLY TO PLAY THE CLARINET, just for me, so one day when he came over to eat he brought his clarinet along. I'm not musical myself. I took piano lessons for three years, but I forgot everything I ever learned. Monroe and I went out and bought a nice upright for the boys — Knabe, there's a silent *K* at the beginning of the name — and Roy took lessons for a year but then he quit. Robert refused even to take lessons. Danny took for two years, but he never practiced. Finally the piano teacher said to me, "Mrs. Tarlow, I don't mind continuing with him. It's money in my pocket. But you're wasting your money." So I stopped giving him lessons and the piano just sat there in the living room with nobody touching it. I had it tuned once a year anyway in case somebody came in and wanted to play. I believe in upkeep.

I don't have a musical nature. Monroe didn't have a musical nature. But Billy has a musical nature. After dinner we sat out on my balcony and he said, "OK, I'm going to give you a thrill," and he played something just beautiful while we were sitting there looking out over the little lake and down at the palm trees. He told me what it was. Mozart something. It's the kind of thing that can bring tears to your eyes. I could listen to him all night. The next day the woman next door said to me, "That was gorgeous. I loved listening to it." That's the power of music; it pleases everybody. Sometimes on Sunday afternoons, her husband moves his TV set out to the balcony and listens to his football game, I don't love that. But that's the price you have to pay for living in a condominium instead of in a private house.

Billy made a confession to me: It's harder to play the clarinet once you get dentures. But he sounds terrific to me. After he finished playing his Mozart, he played something fast — "Mairzy Doats." It's not my favorite song, but a bandleader has to know all those songs. He played it to show me that he could still play fast. "I used to go faster. I used to go like a house on fire," he said. He looked so sad I almost went over and sat on his lap and kissed him. "But now my technique has deteriorated."

He could have given Monroe lessons in technique.

In FLORIDA, nobody ever goes to the ocean. In Boston, you can't keep them away. Everybody's always going, Revere, Nantasket, Nahant, the Cape. Cold water — that must be what does it. Here it's like a bathtub. Only the tourists go for that. When I used to have those tête-à-têtes with Marie, before we'd leave Revere, we used to go for a walk on the rocks there by the water even in the middle of the winter after we closed up the house. A crummy little house, green shingles — ugly — but sweet to us. No matter how cold it was, we'd go. What did we care — we had just finished getting all warmed up. I'd be walking along holding her hand and all the cottages were closed up, nobody near us to see us or hear us. "Feeling good?" That's what I always asked her. I'd lean down and push her scarf aside and kiss her on the neck. We had this rule: no hickeys. She'd take off one of her gloves and she'd reach inside my coat and pull up my sweater and my shirt, whatever it was I was wearing, and she'd run her hand along my back — cold hands, warm heart — and she'd ask me the same question; and we'd both get the same answer.

I drove Joyce to Boca so we could go for a walk on the beach, even though she isn't crazy about the beach; and there I was walking along beside her with my arm around her shoulder. And every once in a while I'd move my hand this way and that, to fool around a bit; but that made her nervous. In Florida everybody worries about muggers. You reach a certain age and you start worrying, or maybe it's because so many of them come from New York. So she wants to turn back. I could feel that gritty feeling, sand under my shoes, and it made me think about Marie — how she was game for anything, nothing frightened her. "What are you, under Mafia protection?" I asked her one day. She only laughed and shook her finger at me, like

warning me. Maybe she was. I don't know. She wasn't
even afraid of her husband. "He leads his life and I lead
mine." That's what she told me. There was only one thing
she worried about: that her daughter might get knocked
up.

"That's my story," she said one day when we were sitting on the bed in the cottage letting the kerosene heater
go for a while so the room could warm up before we
stripped for action. "That's my tragedy. Once is enough."
She took precautions and she made me take precautions
too. I didn't care. It was worth it. But nothing like that
was going to get her daughter, twenty years old, a junior
at Emmanuel College, studying to be a teacher. She
showed me her picture. "Don't let my son get near her," I
said. "Don't let him get after her. Premed, a senior at
Tufts."

"Maybe it's worth it. She'll marry a doctor." She
pinches me. "Don't tell me any more. Better shut up. I'm
weakening."

I didn't say, "Don't let me get near her either." I don't
like crudeness like that.

I'T's A BEAUTIFUL TOPAZ, but I never saw a topaz I really liked. I feel the same about all jewelry like that: It
looks like you got it especially for your birthday because

it's such a birthstone. Once, after we first got married, Monroe gave me an opal ring. He must have got a very good deal on it because when I told him opal is one thing I can't wear because it makes my fingers look pale, he wouldn't let me return it. It must have been an item that one of his coat hooks acquired and handed over to him at a nice price. I told him I couldn't wear it. "So put it away," he said, and that's just what I did. I still have it. I wouldn't even give it to my daughter-in-law, even though Robert's wife wears junk like that. For all I know, her mother might have been the original owner, until somebody heisted it away from her. Like mother like daughter. I wouldn't want to offend Billy by asking him to return the topaz and get me something different. I could help him pick it out. At least he'd be able to return his ring, aboveboard. So I've worn it a couple of times, even though it doesn't really go with anything.

I T WOULDN'T HAVE MADE ANY SENSE to buy Joyce a diamond. Monroe must have got her lots of those. Big carats too. I'm not going to rush into competition with that. She's too tactful to wear her diamond now.

"Why don't you ever wear the ring I gave you?" I asked her. "You don't have to wear it every day."

"I wore it last week when I had on my straw-colored

blouse." She looked a little embarrassed. "It doesn't go with a lot of my clothes. I wear so much pink and lime and so many orange tones."

It's true. She does wear lots of bright colors. They all do down here. It goes with the landscape. On the golf course, they look like a bunch of lollipops walking around. That's because they'll all be in the dark soon enough. "I'll wear it at the wedding, you can be sure of that." Joyce runs her hand along on the back of my neck. That's the place for me. It softens me right up, actually hardens me right up is more like it. Marie knew that and Joyce knows it too. Poor Alice, she never even found out, or if she ever did, she forgot it. "I know just where I want to go to buy the wedding rings."

Joyce wants me to wear a wedding ring. "I don't want to wear a ring," I told her. "It slows down my fingering." Instrumentalists don't like to wear rings. Benny Goodman wore a ring sometimes. I've seen pictures. If I played the trumpet, doing all the work with my right hand, I might do the same, but not with a clarinet. I'm no Benny Goodman.

"I'm dying to get to the ring shop," Joyce told me. "Clique on Worth Avenue. They specialize in unusual wedding rings. They don't carry stones, only gold jewelry."

Joyce likes to shop in Palm Beach. She doesn't like the malls, even Jordan Marsh. "I'm used to the best, Miracle

Mile, Fifth Avenue," she said one time. "Why change at
this late date?"

When we get to Clique, the girl who's running the
place is wearing two, maybe it's three wedding rings. "I'm
enchanted that you're getting married at your age," she
says. "So are we," I tell her. The girl tries to make up
Joyce's mind for her. "Take this one," she says. "It's a
knockout."

But Joyce won't buy it. It's too feminine. She wants to
buy herself a ring that has a matching Mr. model, but she
can't because they won't break up pairs. "We don't do
divorces here," the girl says. "Only weddings." So Joyce
ends up with a ring that's plain. "And lightweight," she
says. "Just in case you do eventually decide that you want
to have one made up. But I tell her I won't decide to. Forget it.

So now we have the wedding ring. $325. The topaz was
$1,295. Two can live as cheaply as one, that's what they say.

THERE'S NO DENYING IT, we had different kinds of
lives. Somebody once told me that Commonwealth Avenue, Brighton, is like Queens, but not so new. Billy's
never even been to Europe. He's been to the Caribbean
only once, after his wife died, and that was a cruise he got
free because he was part of the band. "I thought I was the

one who had died and gone to heaven." That's how he describes it. A singles cruise: He had his pick. Maybe I'll surprise him with a trip to Paris, even if it's the groom who's supposed to pay for the honeymoon. Maybe I just won't even tell him about it and get the tickets myself. He should see Europe.

It's not fair that I should have been so many times and he's never even been. Every year, when Monroe went to the fur show in Frankfurt, West Germany, I'd go along, but I wouldn't go to the show with him. You couldn't get me even to set foot in Germany. Germany gives me the creeps. Paris. That's where I'd stay. One year with my sister-in-law, one year without her — I'm not timid — and so on. That's where I had my once-in-a-lifetime fling. At least I thought it was once in a lifetime. I didn't know I'd ever meet someone like Billy.

Roy leaves, we get the wedding ring, we go to bed and I start showing my age.

"Don't worry about it," Joyce tells me. "Big deal. I like you just the way you are."

"That's not the way I am," I said. "If it is, I don't like me that way." How many times have I laughed at jokes about old men in bed?

The next afternoon, everything returns to normal.

"See," Joyce says to me. "I told you to stop worrying about it."

But the next day again: trouble.

"Am I doing something wrong?" Joyce asked me.

"No," I told her. "I am."

"Come on," she says, and she scrambles down to the foot of the bed and gets me into the position she wants, me lying down with my rear end on her lap and my crotch front and center. Then her hands start going to work on me. "Sometimes this used to be effective with Monroe."

"Did Monroe have trouble from time to time?" It's not right for me to ask. It's none of my business. But I wanted to know.

"Once he got sick, Monroe had chronic problems."

Maybe it was the idea that she'd done this with Monroe, maybe it was me, but whatever it was, no soap. The more she worked at it, the more embarrassed I got.

After a while I go home and I get out the clarinet and I go out on my own balcony and I look out and see the moon and I start playing "Paper Moon." It's not much comfort. I switch to "The Girl That I Marry" and then I slide into "Stormy Weather." I'm not planning to see Joyce the next day. She's got a date with some women to go down to Miami to see a matinee, *Man of La Mancha*. She's having her matinee. Why shouldn't I have mine?

$1,295 on the topaz ring, $325 on the wedding ring.

Another hundred won't kill me. All you have to do is look in the yellow pages under "Escort Service." Friendly, that's the name they were talking about in the exercise room. "She's got to be young," I told them. "And she's got to be stacked." What kind of complexion do I like, they wanted to know. That meant: white or black? "So long as she's white," I said and then after thinking a minute, I told them, "Italian looking." That meant I'd get a Spanish girl, but so what.

She came up in the morning at 11:00 A.M. I was right: Spanish, named Connie and worth every nickel because with her I was like my old self again. First time I ever paid for it, except once when I was in college, just for the experience. Last time I'm ever going to pay for it too, but you're supposed to have a final fling before you get married and what Joyce doesn't know won't hurt her.

I asked her, was she Cuban. Mmm, she goes. If I want Cuban, that's what she'll be for me. Then I asked her what's Connie short for. "Concepción," she says, with a straight face. "It's a good thing you carry around protection with you," I told her. "When's Mother's Day?" She smiles a little just to be agreeable, but I think she didn't get it. Stacked, but not so smart.

The next day and the next day after that, Joyce is wearing the topaz ring. It looks good on her.

I DON'T KNOW WHAT STEPHANOTIS IS, but that's what I plan to carry at the wedding. Stephanotis and lilies of the valley — that's what brides in the society page always carry. I lived all those years in Flower Hill and the only flowers I can recognize are tulips and roses and daisies. In Florida they have all different flowers anyway. Even the grass is different here because they laid it down all at once and it hasn't completely caught on yet. It's the same kind of grass they use in cemeteries, turf. They roll it out over the coffin after funerals so nobody can see how new the grave is. Here they roll it out under your window. It gives me the creeps. It feels like a sponge when you walk on it, as if you'd sink in if you pressed down too hard. We'll all sink in someday, but I'd soon wait as long as possible. Still, the climate is worth a million dollars, even in summer, even with the bugs, bugs like I never saw before. On Long Island we didn't have so many different bugs.

But you learn to adapt. In Florida I've become very adaptable. Who could imagine that someday I'd be going to bed with a man I wasn't even married to, not married to yet that is? Me, who had such a moral upbringing and who was always so faithful to Monroe, never even looking at another man, never straying or fooling around, except only once — well, maybe once and a half.

Roy called me up. He called me at my apartment. He didn't take the precaution of going through his mother to get in touch with me. He dialed direct. "Listen," he says. "Listen good."

"I'm listening," I tell him. "Somebody calls me up on the telephone, I listen. Naturally."

"I read an article in *The Times* real estate section. Boston property values." I don't say a word. I'm listening. "They're going through the roof. You're sitting on a gold mine there."

"That's good to know," I tell him.

"You condo those apartments now, you stand to make a hundred K on every goddamn one of them. At least a hundred K." I can hear his voice, clear as crystal. Money, money. No noise in the room. No interference from the air conditioning. That's because I turn off my air conditioning whenever I can because I don't like the sound. I'm not wild about the smell either. But I hold off on opening the windows for a while to keep the coolness in. So it's quiet, even though it's getting a little stuffy in the house. "You got twenty-eight apartments there," Roy says. "No mortgage to pay off. That's two and a half million clear for you after — repeat after — you deduct the cost of condo-ing."

"How do you know there's twenty-eight apartments?" I'm very suspicious of Roy. He hasn't yet sent back the prenuptial agreement for Joyce to sign. What's he trying to do? Cut his own slice out of that two and a half million dollars?

"Twenty-eight is the number you told me."

"How do you know I paid off my mortgage?"

Roy's quiet for a minute. Then he says, "My mother told me?"

"Is that the kind of thing you talk about with your mommy?" I was getting mad.

"Look," he says. "I admit it. I did some research. As soon as I read this article, that's what turned me on. I'll have my girl run off a copy and send it down to you. It'll really start your juices going. There's this buddy of mine who wants in too. All he takes is five percent of gross. He's been doing the same work here in the city for ten, maybe fifteen years."

Just me, Roy, and the buddy. Both of them take a good cut.

"My own daughter-in-law is in real estate," I say. That stops Roy, but only for a minute. "Then I'll have the girl shoot the copy right down to you today," he says. "And this guy's card too. He's had a lot of experience with tough cases."

Money, money. That's not what gets my juices going. "Don't ever evict me." That gets my juices going.

"Don't ever evict me." Lois's words. "Don't ever let Alice evict me."

I don't even know if Lois is still living in that apartment.

SOMETHING BILLY SAID kind of upset me yesterday. He was sitting beside me in Boca Mall having a cup of coffee after we picked out the stationery for the wedding invitations. We're not going to have them printed up. That's silly at our age. I'll get this artist I heard about in Palm Beach to write them out, calligraphy. It'll be beautiful.

"Roy's really gung ho to make a buck, isn't he!" Billy said. It really startled me. Just like that! Out of the blue.

"Roy always was a businessman." That was the only answer I could think of to give him.

Then Billy told me he had serious doubts about going along with Roy's proposition. I didn't even know what he was talking about.

That's how I heard about Roy's phone call.

"Why doesn't he go through you?" Billy wanted to know. "What's he doing calling me direct?"

So I called Roy myself.

"Your boyfriend's somebody who's got to be goosed into action," Roy said to me. What was I going to do? Tell him that such has not been my experience? That's not something a mother can say to her son.

"Update those apartments," Roy said. "Update him!"

"What are you getting so involved for, Roy?" I felt I ought to know.

Roy's explanation was this: He wants to make sure Billy will support me in the manner to which I'm accustomed.

"At this stage of his life, Billy doesn't want to fiddle around with those apartments," I told Roy. "He doesn't have to. Besides, I don't need Billy to support me."

"What are you, a feminist now?" This is the way my own son talks to his mother. "Can't he pay the bills?"

"Of course he can pay the bills." What else was I going to say to him? No, Billy can't pay the bills.

"One thing I'm going to tell you about your boy-friend." Roy was using that awful I-know-better-than-you voice of his. I used to hear that voice all the time. Monroe used to get it from him even worse. "And this," he said, "is the last word you'll ever hear out of me on the subject: Your boyfriend . . ." He stopped for a minute. Very dramatic. "Billy . . ." Another stop. Then comes the punch line: "Your boyfriend doesn't know how to live the big-ticket life."

It almost made me feel like crying.

"THE HONEYMOON'S ON ME." That's what Joyce said. "You shut your eyes, you hold on to my hand and follow me. Don't worry about anything. I'll give you one hint about it and this is all I'm going to tell you: You need a passport. It takes three or four weeks to get a passport." Then she says — I guess she couldn't resist it — "I'll give you only one more hint about it," and she starts singing. Joyce has a pretty good voice. At least she can carry a tune. That's half the battle: First, you open your mouth wide to let the song get out and, second, you hit the right notes. Presto: you're a good singer. "How would you like to be down by the Seine with me?" That's what she was singing.

I don't want to go to Europe. I traveled enough with the songs. "Under the Bridges of Paris." "April in Portugal." "Arrividerci Roma." For me, the British Museum has lost its charm. I don't want to be an old fart stick-in-the-mud, that's not what I'm developing into. I got myself all the way down here. Alice never even left the apartment. I'm not like that. But I don't want to go to Europe. On a honeymoon, a man should enjoy himself, and I wouldn't enjoy it. Of course, we had the best part of the honeymoon already.

In New York they don't know how to have fun without spending money. There's one thing I know: The best things in life are free. But I have to come up with a different idea for the honeymoon. I was thinking of one of those hotels that are all set up for honeymooners in the Pocono Mountains. Of course, those places pull a young crowd and we'd probably be out of place. But, what the hell. Why shouldn't we enjoy a heart-shaped bed too? A good band? Dancing?

Roy's right: I am a feminist in one way. I believe a woman should be very independent. I'm not talking about financially — though I'm certainly OK in that department thanks to Monroe. I'm saying that a woman shouldn't depend on a man for her entire social life. It's important to go out on your own. I've made new friends here, Edith, Evelyn, Edna — all of them begin wth *E.* I go up to Palm with Edith just to have lunch sometimes. We even went into Miami to see *Man of La Mancha* — a waste of time. Of course I'm used to Broadway shows, the real thing. I'm glad Billy didn't have to sit through that one.

It would be wrong to have to depend on Billy all the time for entertainment. He has his life — his gym, his exercises — and I have to have mine.

When I was still in New York, I always used to get up and go. I can't tell you how many times I went with the groups when Monroe was still alive: "Russian Costumes" at the Metropolitan Museum, chosen for display by Jacqueline Kennedy. Beautiful! The Museum of Modern Art. The Cloisters. But after Monroe died, I didn't wait for expeditions. I went by myself. You don't need to read a how-to-live-as-a-widow book to know you should do that. Lots of times I'd go to the Metropolitan Museum of Art. Sometimes I'd walk around looking at the art for a long time, and sometimes I'd just look for a little while and then find a nice place to sit. I used to enjoy sitting in

the Arab art room, of all places. It was beautiful — all
tiles — and I'd sit and daydream and look at the flower
designs on the tiles. Very peaceful and quiet. That's what
it means to know how to be alone.

One day when I was in the Arab art room I saw this
man there. One of those big men, sort of dead looking
and puffy in the face, not attractive at all. He was walking
around the room and looking at all the vases and the pot-
tery. Why should a man want to look at those things?
You'd think he'd head for one of the rooms that has
knights and swords in it.

All the time he was walking around the room, he never
once looked at me directly, but I could see it: I was the
main attraction. He didn't dare talk to me though. And I
was careful not to look at him. I didn't want to attract his
attention even more. So he left. Nobody else was in the
room. I was alone, and I started to cry. It surprised me.
Not sobbing, just with tears coming into the corners of
the eyes. That's when I decided I was going to get married
again. Widow wasn't the life for me. And that's when I decided I was going to sell the house and move to Florida. I
put it on the market for 465, and 465 is what it sold for.

I couldn't get Monroe to go to the museum with me. I
used to beg him, "Monroe, drive me to the Cloisters today. We'll sit in the garden there. Monroe, let's go into
town and have lunch in the courtyard of the Museum of
Modern Art." No soap. He'd rather play golf or watch

football on TV. Billy likes his gym, but he likes me better. Whenever I ask him, he's always ready to get up and go. He took me to see the Flagler Museum in Palm Beach. Next week we're going to go to the art museum there.

One thing about Billy: He really knows how to enjoy himself. In ten weeks we'll be married to each other.

On the day I had my thirty-ninth birthday I was playing this wedding. The bride was a real peach, nice and bouncy. Alice was — well, Alice. By the time I got home she'd be fast asleep. We used to go out to the Meadows all the time before we got married or to that place at Norumbega Park, I forget the name. I like dancing. Sometimes when I was playing an affair I'd ask one of the backup men to take over for me — usually Lenny, the saxophone, I worked with him for years — and I'd go down and get one of the old ladies sitting on the side to dance with me, just for the fun of dancing; and then another old lady would cut in on me and all of a sudden I was very popular. I think I got jobs from that more than once. No other bandleader did anything like that. But Alice didn't want to go out dancing. All she wanted to do was sit home and watch TV or visit with her family or have her girlfriends over for canasta. "Let's move," I'd say. "Let's buy a house. Let's invest." Because everybody I was

playing jobs for didn't live in Brighton anymore. They
lived in fancier places. "If we don't do it for ourselves,
let's do it for Mark, for the schools. Brookline. Newton.
Maybe down toward Randolph, Canton." It wasn't just
the schools. It was the girls. Where he was going to
school, Latin School, there weren't any girls. All the girls
were in Brookline and Newton, all the good catches.
That's the sort of thing a mother should worry about, but
in this family it was the father. Well, luckily, nobody had
to worry; he did all right for himself. But Alice didn't
want to move. No, she liked the apartment, the dining
room. It was the first dining room she ever had — turns
out it was the last one too. "I like my dining room," she'd
say. "I'd hate to leave it." "I'll get you another dining
room." I pleaded with her. "This isn't the only dining
room in the world." Then, all of a sudden, one day she
says to me, "Now we got enough put aside so we can buy
the building." "OK," I told her. I was happy she wanted
to do something. Now I'm not sorry. A good location.
Twenty-eight apartments. Good rents. It paid off.

But there it was. I was turning thirty-nine and I said to
myself: It's later than you think. I was still in the pink. I'm
still in the pink now, knock wood. But how did I know
how long that was going to last? There I was, working this
wedding. It was the second wedding for the same family.
I'd done the sister too, the same place, the Copley Plaza;
and after we did the bride cuts the cake, the bride feeds

the groom, the bride kisses the groom, all that garbage, they had the Viennese sweet table. And I was playing a fast number for the older crowd, the parents, to keep them away from the sweet table; or if they can't stay away, at least let them work it off; and there was this dark-haired waitress standing behind the sweet table, cutting up pieces of pastry, handing out the ice cream, all that kind of stuff. And while she's serving, she's moving in time to the music, her hips are swaying and her shoulders are bobbing, and I recognize her: She used to sing with this Italian band when sometimes we'd play these back-to-back affairs at the Kenmore in the old days, or at the Somerset. So I swing into "Bill Bailey" because somewhere in the back of my mind I could almost hear her singing it. In fact, I could remember hearing her singing it, and she starts humming along standing there behind the sweet table and finally I point the clarinet at her and I jiggle it and I start marking time with my hand, and she starts to sing.

And she's good.

First, all the people are astonished and they stop dancing and start staring because they aren't accustomed to having singers at weddings. At Italian weddings, sometimes yes. At Greek weddings. But not at Jewish weddings. But they decide, so what. They're enjoying it and soon some of them start dancing again. So when she finished "Bill Bailey," I swing right into "Oh, Marie" because

I figure, being Italian, she'll certainly know that one; and she belts right into it. That's not a song you can dance to — maybe they do the tarantella to it, I don't know, but not ordinary dancing — and so they're all standing there or sitting there listening to her and looking at her; and she is something nice to look at — short but not fat, maybe kind of chunky. If the bride looks so good on her twentieth wedding anniversary, she'll be lucky, but that bride was going to put on weight, I could tell. And after she finishes "Oh, Marie," she winks and shakes her head at me: No more singing. So I start them up dancing again and here's what I start playing: "Enjoy Yourself (It's Later Than You Think)"; and I'm looking right at her and I blow her a kiss and I wink and I shoot at her with my finger, pointing, and she gets the message and winks back and she puckers up her lips and sends me a kiss right back, without blowing it on her hand, but straight out, a regular kiss.

I didn't know it but that was her name: Marie.

That's how it started, the best thing in my life before Joyce. And just when I was worried I was going over the hill.

I'M READY TO SIGN THE PRENUPTIAL, get it over with, but Roy wants Lenny to take another look at it before it's signed, to make sure about the Ginnie Mae bonds and the

taxes. When I go, so much is going to be taken out in
taxes that I shudder to think of it. And then Roy has to
have everything double- and triple-checked. He always
was that way, cautious. Even when he was a kid, he
wouldn't go out and climb a tree like the other boys did;
he had to test the waters first. "What's holding them up?"
Billy asked me the other day when we were down at my
mailbox picking up the mail. The prenuptial wasn't there
yet. I don't want to have to spend my days thinking about
that kind of thing and neither does Billy. It puts a crimp
in my plans. It puts a crimp in everything. We're spending
as much time together, but we aren't getting together as
much this month as we did last month. I notice it. Maybe
you can blame that on getting used to each other, or getting older. Billy's getting older. Now — you can see it —
he shows his age every once in a while. But still he's wonderful. I couldn't ask for anyone better.

It's no wonder that the women around here are so sweet
on him. They'd love to get their hooks into him and not
let go. I suppose he's susceptible. Any man would be. The
one thing that really puzzles me though is how he can pay
any attention to that Rose. She sent him an invitation and
Billy left it around lying right on the bathroom sink,
where he knew I was bound to see it. Maybe he was trying to make me jealous. But as soon as I spotted the sig-
nature, Rose Gruen, I stopped worrying. She's nobody to
be jealous of, the last one I'd pick to interest him. No figure left at all, not exactly fat but more like what you'd call

bulky. I don't go down to the pool so I don't see what's going on there. Maybe I should go from time to time to check out what he sees in them. That one — Rose has a lot of nerve even getting into a bathing suit. Just from looking at her in clothes, you know it's a mistake.

A little note card with flowers on it — forget-me-nots, that's what it said on the back. Inside there was printing: An invitation. And under that she wrote: Dinner Chez Moi, Tuesday the twelfth, at six. A few friends coming over. R.S.V.P., and then her name and phone number. No men friends, I bet. Just women. He must have RSVP'd no, because he was with me the next Tuesday at six. But there'll be other invitations. You can bet on it.

J OYCE WANTS ME TO GET A MANICURE. I told her absolutely no. First the wedding ring, then the manicure. She has a hard time leaving my hands alone. There's nothing wrong with my hands. I never had any complaints about my hands before. Her son gets his hands manicured. I can see it: His fingernails are filed even, absolutely even; I never saw anything like it before. Not for me, that's not my style. Too Liberace for me. They even shine a little bit, his fingernails, not from nail polish, I hope that's not the reason, maybe just from buffing.

He's back in Florida, Roy. Another visit. It isn't that he can't stay away from his mommy. It's me he can't stay

away from. It's my building on Commonwealth Avenue
he wants to get near. I was tempted to lace into him, but
I didn't want to upset Joyce. She'd be sure to hear about it
too. I said to him, "When are you going to send back the
prenuptial, Roy? You're really holding up the works."

Roy doesn't bat an eyelash. Instead he starts talking
about my building. "Too bad you didn't come down next
week instead of now," I told him. "That's when my
daughter-in-law is going to be here. She's the one who's in
real estate. If there's any condoing going on, she'll be the
one to handle it, not you." I look him straight in the eye.
"Not that there's going to be any condos. Not while I have
a say in the matter." I can see his mind working. Joyce and
I get married, even before we sign the prenuptial. We can't
wait, like we're kids hot to trot. I pop off. Joyce ends up
with the building and Roy starts condoing. He's the one
who makes I don't know how many grand on it. That's
the way Roy's thinking.

Would you believe it, he flies back home on Thursday
because he suddenly remembers he's got a business appointment the next day and he arranges to come back
down again next week after Margery gets here.

BILLY'S DAUGHTER-IN-LAW IS NAMED MARGERY, a
lovely girl with red hair, but a soft color, and beautifully
dressed. She's here with his grandson, Jeffrey, twelve years

old, smart as a whip. Jeffrey's got the message: They came here to look me over. That makes sense. The family should see what's going on. Margery's very tactful while she's looking me over, and she likes what she sees, I can tell that. But the kid has sex on the brain. He eyes me like I was a girl his age, like he's trying to figure out what the old man's getting turned on about. At that age, they're just learning.

"Jeffrey," I said to him. "Do you want me to show you the crafts room?" I go there myself from time to time when my own grandchildren come down. It keeps them amused because they can't spend all their time in the pool, even though they'd like to. I wouldn't go to the crafts room for myself, a bunch of widows making these ugly vases shaped like cowboy boots. The boots are all there already. All you have to do is glaze and fire them. I don't call that creative if it's shaped already. And they have these wine goblets already made out of clay. They can take these goblets and twist the stems and that's supposed to make them look prettier. I think it only makes them look drunk. That's the sort of thing they do in the crafts room. But it keeps them busy. My grandchildren too.

Not Jeffrey. He wants the pool and his mother lets him stay in the pool. Billy's got a lot of patience with him. The second day Jeffrey was here, the two of them threw a Frisbee back and forth for a solid three-quarters of an hour. I clocked them. Normally, I wouldn't do something like that, but I was so amazed by how long they played Frisbee the first day that I just wanted to see how long they could keep it up. I should have known Billy had that kind of staying power.

All the time they were playing, I was sitting by the pool talking to Margery, asking her about the work she does. She doesn't just sell houses. She also manages apartment buildings like the one Billy owns. "I bet you'll enjoy talking to my son Roy," I said to her. "He's coming down again before you go back to Boston." She already knew about Roy because Billy mentioned him to her. I hope the two of them can make their arrangements without bothering Billy. He's got lots of talents, but he's not a businessman.

I took Margery up to my apartment to show her what I'm planning to wear at the wedding. She thought it was gorgeous, especially the blouse. She's going to wear a summer silk dress, tailored. Straw-colored. That's the way they dress in Boston. Maybe she picked that color because she's got reddish hair, very light. She's the type who could wear a topaz ring. Maybe that's what they wear in Boston — topaz rings.

Roy ARRIVED AGAIN YESTERDAY and took my daughter-in-law out to lunch. "What's going on?" I asked her.

"What are you cooking up together?" "Don't worry about
it," she said. "He's someone who likes to hear the sound of
his own voice so I let him talk and I listen. But it doesn't
mean a lot. There's nothing to worry about." So I'm not
worrying. In fact I'm glad she's here to take Roy off my
back.

Besides, I'm having enough trouble keeping up with
Jeffrey. First we were just tossing the Frisbee back and
forth nice and easy. But then he figured he ought to put
the old man on the spot, so he started angling the Frisbee
until it went a little bit to one side and then a bit to the
other side, every way but straight. He's really good at it,
an athletic kid. And then every once in a while when I
wasn't expecting it, he'd fire it straight on, hard. He
learned how to do that. Ferocious! like we were playing at
Wimbledon. The kid's a John McEnroe. "Hey, Jeffrey,
"don't play so hard with Grandpa," Margery yelled out at
him one time. Even Joyce looked a little concerned.
Maybe she was worried I'd have a heart attack running
around like that in the sun. "Easy! Easy!" she kept saying.
"Easy, Billy, easy." But if I'm going to go, that's the way I
want to do it — a coronary, while I'm having fun. Not
necessarily when I'm in the saddle. That's not for me; too
many jokes about that situation. But someday when I'm
just fooling around having a good time, that's a different story.

Yesterday i drove to palm and got the artist — I should say, commissioned the artist — to do the calligraphy. Nine more weeks and that's it. I'm a married woman again. Roy had better show up with the prenuptial in his hand when he comes down to see me this time or else I'm in trouble. I can smell it.

Once when i was playing a wedding, the groom's father ups and has a heart attack while he's dancing. He didn't die right there though; he waited until he got to the hospital. I was playing "Sentimental Journey" — "Going to set my heart at ease," and *poof* — quick as that. He sort of gurgles and he's holding on to his throat and he slouches down onto the lady he's dancing with — I don't know, maybe it was his own wife. She screams. He topples over. Everybody's screaming. The bride's screaming. She's as white as her gown. "Mickey!" people are yelling. "Mickey!" Later I find out Mickey's not the father. Mickey's this relative who's a doctor. Mickey gets up from his table. He runs over and starts slapping the father's face. The bride is still screaming. Somebody runs out to call an ambulance. "Heart attack," they're whispering. "What a tragedy."

I don't know what to do. I send the bass player down to

get me a drink. He comes back with a double scotch, more than I want, but in this situation, it's OK. They're all looking at me like I should be doing something. What's next? "Go Get the Stretcher, Baby. I Ain't Going to Last." I don't know that number. Maybe "Waiting for the Ambulance?" "What the hell do we do?" I say to Marty Fish, the saxophonist. "What do we do? 'The Star Spangled Banner'?" Marty's no help. "Glory, Glory, Hallelujah," he tells me. Every number I can think of in mood music is the wrong selection. "Beyond the Blue Horizon." "There's a Happy Land Somewhere." Finally, I figure I've got to do something. I'm being paid by the hour. So I start out very soft with "Dream, When You're Feeling Blue." Then I slide into "Accentuate the Positive." And believe it or not, the groom takes hold of the bride — his own father is lying there flat out on the dance floor — and he puts his arms around her and sort of rocks her, not exactly dancing, but not exactly not dancing either. There's two or three old ladies sobbing and wiping their faces with their napkins; and one of them shouts out, "Stop it, Michael! Stop dancing!" She stands up and shakes her napkin at him. "Respect!" she shouts, but another old lady shushes her up, and Michael keeps on dancing until they come in with the stretcher and wheel the old man out.

All I'm doing is sliding back and forth between "Dream" and "Accentuate the Positive." That's all I can think of until the bride's father comes over to pay me off. When he's writing out the check, he looks at his watch. 10:30. He only pays me up until eleven — big sport — and I don't have the heart to remind him that the contract says till twelve and by rights that's how he should pay. But he's got enough troubles. I wonder how long that marriage lasted. The next day it was in the paper: The old man died. I should have been playing "The Funeral March."

That's why I believe in live now, pay later. Later, there's no more dancing, no more accentuating the positive.

WHEN I GET TO BE AN OLD LADY, I'm not going to fight it. I'm going to grow old graciously, unlike some of the people around here. I try not to feel old but I can't kid myself, it's creeping up on me. My neck shows it. I try to keep my chin down whenever Billy sees me without clothes on. He must think I'm crazy the way I look at him with the top half of my eyes, like I was flirting with him. Maybe he thinks I'm having trouble with my vision. (I am, but that's another story.)

Billy is always fighting it. He can't accept the changes that are coming over his body. That's why he spends every day at the gym. Sometimes he has a one-track mind. I suppose I shouldn't complain when I look around and see all the women here, widows, without any men at all. Billy's always trying to act like a teenager, international, as we used to say in high school — Roman hands and Russian fingers.

No QUESTION ABOUT IT. I'm slowing down. That happens to the best of them, the best of us I should say. Around the gym, they're all making jokes. "Did you get it up this month, Milt? Not even once?" That sort of thing. They think it's funny. I don't think it's so funny.

Last week another time — that was the second or third time it happened — Joyce caught me out showing my age. Embarrassing. "I don't mind at all," she said. "You don't believe it, but it's you I care about, not your performance, so-called." If Joyce doesn't mind, why does she get so happy when things are going fine? I didn't point out the discrepancy. Why should I? Saturday, everything was OK. Monday morning, it was like old times with Marie. Even better than with Marie, except for the fact that I was getting nervous. And then yesterday, we were in her place just like usual, it was nice and quiet, Margery and Jeffrey had gone away to Monkey Jungle for the day; Roy wasn't in my hair, he was down in North Miami Beach visiting some friends of his; but privacy didn't make any difference at all. Even so: trouble again. That's the third or fourth time it happened. I'm losing count.

"Give yourself some time to recover. Restore your strength." That's the word at the gym. Old men's wisdom. "You don't have to swing more than once a week." Poor Milt — Ellis, that's his last name. There's no reason why I should keep his name out of it. He doesn't seem to mind. He's the butt of the jokes because he keeps telling all these stories about what an operator he used to be. He can't keep quiet about it. If he kept his mouth shut, they wouldn't ride him so much. He can't do it anymore, so he spends all his time talking about it. That must be what they mean when they say dirty old man. He never shuts up. He's a talkaholic. I could probably tell just as many stories, but that's not my style.

Just as many stories? Well, maybe not. I always went for quality not quantity. But still, I used to worry: Was I a fuckaholic? There were some times when I couldn't get enough of it. Marie in the afternoon, and then I'd come home and with Alice it was like I never even heard of Marie. I was that wild. One day, and this is the absolute truth, after I got together with Lois, I did it three times: morning, afternoon, and night.

That's because Lois lived right in my building and, in the morning after she finished getting her kids off to school, it was clear sailing. Alice didn't pay any attention to me, not in daylight hours anyway, so I could ring Lois's doorbell if I wanted to — she lived on the second floor — on my way downstairs, and stop in on her. Get right in the door, hush, hush, very secret, and if anybody saw me going into the apartment, they could think I was there collecting rent or fixing something — what did they know?

I was collecting it all right. I was fixing something. Every Tuesday morning. We had a regular date. Plus Marie twice a week. Plus Alice, whenever. That's what I mean fuckaholic. I needed to have it, like a drinker. I couldn't do without it. Bang. Bang. Bang. Maybe that was my midlife crisis, like you read about. They're trying to prove to themselves that they're still all there. Well, no question about it: I was all there.

Finally, though, I told myself, This is crazy. Slow down. A married man. Forty-two years old. It's wrong to be so wrapped up in one thing, as if there's nothing else going on in the world. So I started to cool off a little bit with Lois. I kept on with Marie, but Lois and I, eventually we cut loose. Not that Alice suspected anything — I don't think she would have cared even — but I got the feeling Lois wanted out. I think she was getting tired of it. One morning she told me, "I'm worried your wife is getting suspicious. I saw her in the laundry and she gave me this really funny look." Then about a week later, she said, "I think my husband is getting suspicious too. Yesterday he came home from work in the middle of the afternoon, just like that, no reason, he just showed up." My ego wasn't hurt, a beautiful girl, dark hair, dark complexion, big boobs, hips like battleships. Very squeezable; but I was ready to slow down. Marie was plenty enough for me. And Alice too, of course.

And now Joyce is plenty. I don't think I could handle another one, even if the loveliest girl in the world came along. To me right now that's who Joyce is: the loveliest girl in the world. I'm lucky.

ROY CAME DOWN AGAIN YESTERDAY, along with a friend of his. They talked to the daughter-in-law. Roy got the impression that she's a very sensible girl. I hope they can work together on the condoing and get Billy to go along. Roy thinks she can manage it.

Here's what Billy said the day before Roy got here: "If I had to do it all over again, I'd still play the clarinet, you betcha." You betcha, that's the way he was talking, like a hayseed. "But," he said, "I'd also learn how to do skywriting. I'd get up in my airplane and I'd juice up my smoke machine and do you know what I'd write?" I didn't know. How could I guess what he'd write? If I were going to guess, knowing Billy, I'd guess something about sex. Something like, Let's do it, baby! Sex is what he's got on his mind all the time. I never saw anything like it. He's a man who's going to go out fighting, I'll tell you that.

He could hardly wait to tell me what he'd write. Like a kid, he was so excited. And I mean excited. He said he'd

write: I LOVE YOU, JOYCE. He'd fly right over my house
in Flower Hill and write I LOVE YOU, JOYCE in the sky
so they could see it all over Long Island. I LOVE YOU,
JOYCE. Isn't that sweet?

That's the kind of man he is. Not what you'd call
down-to-earth. But still, hard to resist.

Roy still didn't bring the prenuptial agreement back
down here with him. It's right on his desk, he says, but he
forgot it rushing to catch the plane. He forgot it. I'll bet.

AFTER WE OWNED OUR BUILDING TWELVE, fourteen
years, one day we're driving out to see Alice's sister in
Newton — a spring day — the trees are popping out in
flowers all up and down Commonwealth Avenue. The
same street we live on, but a world of difference. Houses
versus apartment buildings. Dogwood trees versus trolley
tracks. I played some of those houses. They have big yards
in back, and they'd set up tents and dance floors for their
affairs and then pray to God that it wouldn't rain or be
too sweltering and then they'd have their affair and hully-
gully like anybody else. The thing was this: They had
more money than anybody else and they didn't have to
pay the rent on a hall. They saved money.

Alice always was jealous of her sister who married a
lawyer, but she held it in. We're driving along to visit the

sister and Alice is going "Mmmm" and "Oooh" whenever she sees a tree she likes, and then suddenly in the middle of everything, out of the blue, she says: "OK. We've got $106,000 cash. I'll put twenty-five down on a house, we'll put it in Mark's name, no inheritance tax, and we move. We rent out the apartment we're in now and it pays the mortgage for us."

I almost crashed the car. For years I'm pleading with her, "Move! Move!" Now all of a sudden she's ready to move.

She didn't say anything to her sister. That wasn't Alice's way. But she started looking at the real estate ads. In fact the day I found her after her heart attack, there she was fallen down in front of the sofa with the trolley going by and her face flat down on the floor on top of *The Globe* — the real estate section. That was the first time I ever saw a dead body.

That's Roy's favorite reading matter — *The Globe* real estate section. I always used to look at the wedding announcements to see write-ups of the affairs I played at. Now it will say: JOYCE TARLOW WEDS BANDLEADER. In a few months. March 16. Read all about it!

[II]

Rose and Billy

I NEVER LEARNED how to drive but I learned how to walk. Therefore I do a lot of walking. Everybody kept telling me: Rose, you ought to take driving lessons. Rose, you should get your driver's license. But I never got around to doing it. And now that I'm in my seventies, it's too late to start.

The other morning I was heading for the drugstore to get some exercise and to buy some Diet-Aid. I could have taken the Daymoor Village jitney on its morning shopping trip. I could have hitched rides with Ethel or with May. Both of them stopped to offer me a ride while I was outside the Entertainment Center, right under those ugly decorations — if you can call them decorations — the smile mask for comedy and the gloomy mask for tragedy, with the corners of its mouth turned down. But I kept on walking. Exercise, exercise, I told myself. I was under the banyan trees, almost at the gateway where I have to go outside the Village boundaries to cross the highway — if

the cars don't kill you there, the carbon monoxide can —
when Billy stopped his car and said, "Hey, cutie, want a
ride?" My heart went pitter-patter. This is one item I'll
have to write down in my diary, I said to myself. This was
an offer I couldn't refuse and I hopped right into his car.

I know I'm no cutie. Too old, too tall, too gray, too
overweight. At the Entertainment Center I'd fit right in
with the performers they get to appear there, outmoded
stars singing songs that were popular a long time ago. But
I'm always glad to flirt. "Where are you heading?" Billy
asked me. He himself was going to the barber. He's got a
beautiful head of hair. Almost no gray. I wish I could say
the same. But the hair on his chest is gray. On him it looks
good. Every time I see him come out of the pool and
shake himself dry, my heart shakes too.

Eighty-four degrees is what the big time-and-tempera-
ture clock outside the drugstore read: 1030. 10:30 a.t., Adventure Time. "Let's synchronize our watches," Billy said.
"Does an hour give you enough time?"

"Plenty," I told him, and we arranged to meet inside
the drugstore in an hour. At the shampoo counter, right
by the hair lighteners. I picked the spot. "Gentlemen pre-
fer blonds," I said. Very bold, but why should I worry?
More than one person has reported it: Every morning by
the dawn's early light Billy can be seen leaving Joyce Tarlow's condo, and she is very blond. Florida is wall-to-wall
blonds. "Maybe I'll dye my hair," I said.

"You'd look good blond," he told me. "Not that you don't look good as is." And then he drove off to tend to his own hair.

As is! Whoever gets me is going to have to take me as is. That is if anyone is ever going to get me.

One hour. First I bought my Diet-Aid. Then I hung around looking at newspaper headlines. Arms Control. Russians. Et cetera. There was no reason at all for me to plunk down thirty-five cents to buy a newspaper when every morning my next-door neighbors leave yesterday's paper outside for me. Every day, day after day. Really important news shows up on TV anyway on the day it happens, first on the five o'clock news and then on the six and seven; and then, even if I don't stay up to watch, again on the ten o'clock and the eleven.

Then I moved on to the bookstore, or to what passes for a bookstore here in FL. Lots of paperbacks with raised letters on their covers. Lots of magazines: *Golden Age, Golden Years, Young at Heart.* Plus *Florida Fun* and *Senior Years* and *Senior Fun.* WIDOWHOOD CAN'T KILL YOU! one of the covers said. Meanwhile, I'm a widow and I walk around half dead. IMPOTENCE DOESN'T HAVE TO RUIN YOUR LIFE! Easy for them to say. Reading them all could use up a person's entire old age, including second childhood.

Nobody I knew was in the store. There was a good-looking man, tall, with white hair, holding a book in his

hand and a leash with a dog attached to it. I never was the
kind of person who could go up to a man and say, "What
are you reading?" I wish I were. Maybe I could have made
friends with the dog. It looked bored. They say animals
have no sense of the future. Not this dog. He'd been told:
"Wait," and he was waiting for what the future would
bring. He had perfect posture. Most humans don't. They
carry themselves poorly — except for certain young men
I've seen on TV, standing on street corners getting ready
to hurl rocks. But these boys aren't really waiting. They're
tired of waiting. That's why they throw rocks. I was tired
of waiting. I could feel myself slouching. Maybe I could
have hurled a book at the man. That would get his attention. Twenty more minutes. There was no place to sit
down, except on a little step stool. My feet hurt. How
long can you browse in a bookstore anyway?

WHAM BAM! — I was in and out of that barbershop in
fifteen minutes. Now I have all this time to kill before I
pick up Rose at the drugstore. And in this hot weather too
when I could be hanging around the pool instead. Joyce
never goes to the pool. This is why: She says she's never
found a bathing cap that looks good on her. And she's got
another reason: There are all old ladies down there. Why
should she hang out with them, she says. I don't mind
hanging out with them: Some of them aren't that old.

I love to watch them during the exercise class. A couple of them are real walruses — they need whatever exercise they can get; for them the best exercise would be walking away from the dinner table — but aside from the walruses, the others are fun to watch. No real beauties but some nice-looking gals. They're making the most out of their declining years. You can see it: Old age is no fun. But they're game about it. No bikinis but they do what they can with what they've got. Rose is in the class; she wears a bathing suit with a big red flower across one breast, it looks like Christmas. "What's that?" I asked her once. I pointed at it. No joke intended. I just wanted to know what kind of flower it was. "A poinsettia," she said to me. "Gift wrapping."

They have a new exercise director now, Marty. They all love him. They used to have Phil, a guy who lived at Daymoor, but one day — just like that — pop! — Phil ups and dies on them. So then they got another guy from Daymoor, Bernie. But he didn't work out. The old ladies hated him. One-two-three-four! His counts sounded like they were being shot out of a gun. "Too fast, Bernie," they yelled at him. I could hear them complaining. "Slow down." And "What does he want to do, kill us?" So they got rid of him, and somewhere they found an old tape recording of Phil running the class and they started using that instead, a dead man's voice coming to them from beyond the grave. But then one day Marty came to Daymoor looking for work because he needed money after his daughter matriculated — his word, matriculated — at the University of Miami. So they hired him, and now everybody's happy.

But I'm not so happy because meanwhile I'm not at the pool. I'm stuck out here in this heat killing time until I pick up Rose.

THE TEMPERATURE OUTDOORS went up to 87°, but inside the drugstore it was plenty cool. I went over to the hair-care aisle. No surprises there: A blond rinse. A conditioner guaranteed to add bounce to the hair. For TV models, maybe. For widows, no. A new Swedish shampoo looked tempting, but it was too heavy for me to carry around. They had one bottle for dark hair and another for light but there was nothing for gray hair. I didn't buy it. I'm never going to bleach my hair. I never wanted to be blond anyway.

At 11:30 exactly, I stationed myself in front of the blond rinse in the hair-care aisle exactly where I told Billy I'd be. But no Billy showed up. I figured there were so many customers in his barbershop that he'd been delayed. 11:35 went by and then 11:40 and still Billy didn't show up. Finally, I went to check on the clock outside. 11:45. 88°. There was a bench out there, and I was really tired, but it would have been dumb to sit outside waiting.

12:00, and still no Billy. I had to make a decision. The Daymoor shopping jitney was outside, and there wouldn't be another one until 2:00 P.M. I started wondering: How old was Billy anyway? He was certainly too young to be forgetful already. Was he standing me up? Should I take this jitney now and let him do the worrying if he doesn't find me? Or should I wait? If Billy didn't appear and I tried to phone for a taxi, it would be like throwing a quarter away. Calling for a taxi in Florida is like calling for a dogsled. Forget it. I decided to wait and I went further inside the drugstore so Mel, the jitney driver, wouldn't spot me.

Some adventure. It had turned sour on me. I was beginning to get mad. I'm too old to be standing on my feet for more than an hour. Then I started worrying: Maybe Billy had a heart attack. Maybe he was in the hospital at that very moment. Maybe he'd run off with another woman. I was getting hungry. It was time for lunch, and I could feel the beginnings of the headache I get if I don't eat on time. I had expected to be home by noon, sitting on my balcony eating lunch, cottage cheese and fruit, not one of those mealy apples they sell here in Florida, but maybe a peach, maybe some grapes; maybe a cucumber or a tomato for a nice change. I tried to remember: How much fruit was there in the refrigerator? Not much, a widow's portion, just enough for a woman living alone. It would have been crazy for me to leave the drugstore and walk over to the supermarket to buy a pint of strawberries. Or maybe some grapes. Crazy.

Food. Sitting down. The other woman. There was nothing else for me to think about. Maybe when Billy finally came, he'd have his suitcase packed, we'd drive south, to the Keys, to a hotel room overlooking a field of poinsettias, big and red and in full bloom. 12:24. No Billy. 12:26. 12:28. Suddenly Billy appeared, one hour late. "Here I am. Right on time," he said.

I bit my lip. But then I blurted it out. "I thought we agreed on eleven-thirty."

Billy looked at his watch. "Twelve-thirty," he said. "Just like I promised." He patted my arm. I was sweaty. "Twelve-thirty," he said. "Twelve-thirty, Rose. You're too young and beautiful to be turning forgetful already."

What could I say to him after that?

YESTERDAY, ANOTHER ONE POPPED OFF. I was lying in bed with Joyce and I heard the ambulance siren. "There's the attack squad again," I said. Joyce never thinks that's funny. I tried another one: "Maybe it's the Daymoor Symphony Orchestra." But she wasn't laughing.

Today, down at the pool, I found out who it was. Leon Harrison, the president of the condo association. Only seventy-four years old. So now there's going to be a new election.

There was no vice president to step into his shoes. Who runs for vice president anyway? Nobody. Treasurer, yes. There's always a contest there, but never for vice president.

The last contest for treasurer was between a dress manufacturer and a really rich guy. Of course, the rich guy won. He made his money in plastics. He was the brains behind the hula hoop, that was the rumor. At the pool they're talking, trying to figure it out: Who's going to be the new president? The smart money says it won't be the treasurer. Rich as he is, he's started to get kidney failure and he doesn't have the strength for politics anymore. The dress manufacturer who ran for treasurer before isn't even going to try this one. He turned bitter from losing his last election.

The next day at the pool, the news comes out: A woman is going to run. Lots of jokes about that. And who's the woman? Rose. That Rose, she's incredible. She's got twenty, twenty-five votes just from the gals who have been in and out of her exercise classes over the years. She ran for office before and she won, but that was only against another woman: secretary of the condo association. And now she's going all the way. Joyce doesn't care for her, but I think she's got guts. Not beautiful, but plenty game. She's got my vote.

I HAVE NO REGRETS about getting into this. No matter how old you are you should keep trying new things. I firmly believe that. I'm not doing it just because I don't have a man. The National Organization for Women elected a new president, a woman in her midseventies, and she urged women to run for office. I read that in the newspaper. So I'm running. Call me Rose-evelt. I might even win.

God knows, I'm working hard enough at it. After one of my leaflets got soggy at the pool and the ink ran all over my friend Florence's sea green bathing suit and completely ruined it, I decided I'd better deliver the leaflets door to door. As it turns out, that was a wise decision: It was a first, not only for Marilyn Circle but for all of Daymoor. In all the elections — Tyrone Circle, Errol Circle, Merle Terrace, everywhere — nobody had ever done leafleting like that before. I walk all around, ringing doorbells, and then if nobody answers, I have to bend down to push a leaflet under the door. Not an easy movement for a woman my age.

But the face-to-face meetings can be wonderful. At one door I came across a man, scrawny with a mustache, who lives in the condo right next to my opponent, Parlin; and he told me he's going to vote for me and not for Parlin. That's priceless, and it makes all the bending over worthwhile, even though I had to bend over again when I came to Parlin's own condo because I certainly wasn't going to ring his doorbell. I smelled cigar smoke. I think he was home. When he finds my leaflet, he'll know he's in trouble.

In the same building, one floor up, I came across a fancy brass doorplate: TARLOW. Very showy. She must have brought it down from New York. But a vote's a vote, so I rang. I don't know who was more surprised when Billy answered the door: him or me. I mean, he or I. Handsome! Especially because he was wearing just his bathing suit and a terry-cloth bathrobe.

I handed him a leaflet. I don't mind if he's half naked — all naked would be OK with me — but apparently he was embarrassed because he pulled his belt tighter so I'd see less of him. Blondie came to the door to see who was ringing. After all, it's her condo. She took the leaflet right out of his hand, looked at it for a minute, and told Billy, "She's running against that Parlin, the one who's always smoking cigars," and then she wrinkled her nose as if she smelled something bad. "You've got my vote," she said. Billy chimed right in: "Me too." I'd like it better if he had more independence. Not on this issue, but in general. Me too. Terrible. I hope that's not how he's going to say I do at his wedding. Me too.

"Thank you," I said. "Election day is December 22," and I started making my getaway, but before I could leave, Blondie had her hand out. "Give me some leaflets and I'll pass them out in my canasta group. Eight girls." I

counted out some leaflets for her. Eight, nine, ten — all
of them wasted. She's nothing but a blond bimbo and
she'll forget all about them.

"LET'S GO TO THE CONDO MEETING TONIGHT,
Joyce says to me. "I'd like to see the fireworks."

"What fireworks?" I said.

"Between Rose and that Parlin" was the answer.

So we went. Joyce even wore her topaz ring. These
things never pull crowds. Still, there were maybe fifteen,
twenty people there. Until the new president gets elected,
they have the treasurer running the show. After Rose reads
the minutes from the last meeting, the treasurer calls out:
Any new business? And she stands right up again to make
a motion.

As soon as she said it — "I move that we organize some
all-condo activities" — that's when the fireworks start.
Joyce called it right. I have to give her credit. Parlin stands
right up and says: "Activities! Peh!"

He's a real New Yorker, the way he talks. "Activities is
why we bought. Peh! We don't need more activities."

I'm on Rose's side, but in a way, he's right. There's
enough activities around here to make you dizzy: golf
classes, swimming classes, exercise classes, woodwork-
ing, ceramics, Ping-Pong, billiards, learn Spanish, et
cetera. You name it, they've got it.

"Peh!" Parlin says again. "Ha ha. Activities."

But that wasn't enough to shoot Rose down. She's still standing up and she says, "I'm waiting for a second to the motion I just made." I thought I'd be a sport and second the motion for her, but before I could even open my mouth, I hear her saying: "If nobody wants to second it, I'll make another motion: I move that we have a Marilyn Circle block party."

Nobody seconds that motion either.

You've got to hand it to Rose. She keeps on plugging away. "I think we should have our next installation as a picnic," she says. "We could make it potluck."

That one got to Joyce. "Potluck," she said, like she never heard the words in her entire life. She likes a catered affair. I'm nobody to knock catered affairs. I made a good living out of them for thirty, thirty-five years. All those weddings and bar mitzvahs, plus bat mitzvahs when they started to feature girls. But Joyce feels that spending is the only way to live.

"I'll make another motion," Rose says. "I move that members go on a weekly group expedition outside the walls of Daymoor Village."

I stand right up and second that motion. When I sit down, Joyce leans over and whispers in my ear, "She can't drive a car. That's why she needs people to take her places."

But before the motion can even come to a vote, Parlin is chitchatting with one of his buddies, Al Spear, the guy who's really got the hots for Joyce. He eyeballs her every chance he gets. Parlin reaches into his pocket and pulls out his wallet. "What's that you got there?" Spear asks, like they rehearsed the scene.

Parlin's got the answer all ready. "That's my DNR card."

"What's DNR?" Spear wants to know.

I don't know what DNR is, but I can see it's going to kill Rose's motion. "DNR," the treasurer joins the game. "Do not resuscitate. Are you one?" He sounds swishy when he asks, and then he swishes his hand to make the point. "I'm one too."

Parlin starts passing the card around. I have to admit it: It grabs my interest and I take a good look. DO NOT RE-SUSCITATE it says. TAKE NO HEROIC MEASURES and then it gives Parlin's blood type just in case they want to do some medical work anyway. Rose is just left hanging there. Everybody forgets about her motion. It's not even voted on. DNR — or maybe I should say Parlin — wins the day.

"Don't worry, Rose," I tell her while she's walking out. "You get a couple of friends together and we'll go on a nice expedition."

JOYCE WAS AFRAID to let him go off alone with Jeanette and Pauline and me — too many unattached women —

so she had to come along to chaperone. She's worrying: Is she going to lose her boyfriend? Pauline and Jeanette are worried they're going to get robbed. As soon as Jeanette spotted the Martin Luther King sign she started squealing: "Martin Luther King Boulevard. That's where the race riots were." Not a black face in sight. I'm the only one who's got nothing to worry about. I'll either win my election or I'll lose it. Only two possibilities.

As it turned out, I had plenty to worry about. But I didn't know it then, thank God.

"Don't worry, girls," Billy said when we drove past. "No danger."

I was sitting directly behind him. I could see that it was almost time for him to have another haircut.

The expedition was to Bayside, a very interesting mall. But we weren't allowed to walk around it together. Blondie had to have her own private lunch with Billy. They arranged a time to meet us later. "Today," Billy said to me, "let's synchronize our watches and make sure we agree on the time." Then the three of us had a lunch at a restaurant overlooking the bay. Pauline especially loved it. "It's so beautiful here, like a foreign country," she said. The hell with cholesterol, I decided, and I ordered shrimp salad. It was cheap, but that's because it only had little bits of shrimp cut up in it, not whole shrimp. Then we went wandering around the shops. Very interesting. Imports from Morocco, carvings from Haiti, Guatemalan embroideries, and so on.

Pauline's a real shopper. So is Jeanette. They can spend an hour in just one store looking at everything. Not me. I went on ahead while they dawdled. The further on I got, the more foreign it really did seem. I found myself in one store standing in the middle of a bunch of German tourists. In another store everybody was jabbering away in Spanish, including the shopkeeper. This was a place called Mama Nature — rocks cut open to show amethysts inside, animal skins from pumas, spider monkeys, and I don't know what else, various kinds of endangered species. I felt like a member of an endangered species in there myself, all those foreigners closing in on me. I didn't know whether they were local Cubans or tourists from South America, all of them such an odd color, almost like light coffee; and one girl, maybe she was a young woman — who can tell the age? I can't anymore — wearing the kind of thing I hate, one of those too-tight dresses Spanish women wear, to me they're cheap looking. It made my skin crawl. I got very uncomfortable; I felt I had to get out of there. Right outside the store there was a bench with one of those families sitting on it. They looked like spider monkeys come down from the trees. As soon as I got close to them, they picked themselves up and scrambled away. All of a sudden, as I was heading to the bench, it became hard for me to walk. Maybe I looked drunk, maybe I was staggering. I'd seen some Indian blowguns on sale in one of the stores I walked into. I

thought a foreigner blew a dart at me out of one of those
blowguns and it hit me right in the neck. Can you believe
it? Imagine thinking that. I could actually feel it hitting
me. So when I finally got to the bench, I just sat there and
closed my eyes. My watch was synchronized, but so what?
I didn't care.

W HEN I FINALLY SPOTTED HER, she was sitting on a
bench, eyes closed. Her face was as gray as cardboard. I
didn't have the heart to wake her up. Finally she opened
her eyes and saw me standing there. "I must have fallen
asleep," she said. "How did you find me?"

"I caught you now," I said, just to keep it light. I think
she must have blacked out, but I didn't say anything.
"Wait right here," I told her, "and I'll pick you up. I can
drive up to that door." There was a handicapped-access
door right near the bench. All the time while I was walking her through on the way out to the car I kept my arm
around her. When I got her into the car and Joyce took a
look at her, she was shocked. "Rose, we'll drive you in to
see the doctor," she said. "All you have to do is make the
appointment."

"Oh, it's nothing," Rose said. She kept saying, "It's
nothing, nothing important. Stop worrying about it. I'm
not worrying."

So when no phone call came asking us to take her to a doctor's appointment, I stopped worrying too. You can lead a horse to water, everybody knows that, but that's all you can do. And when I went down to the pool and saw her there looking as good as new with that red flower on her bathing suit, and I said to her, "Rose, how are you feeling now?" she smiled at me and said she was just fine, not to worry, just fine.

I think she didn't want to get into any discussion about her health out there in public because there's a rumor floating around that she's not in the best of health and that she shouldn't even be running in the election. One of the guys at the pool told me that, but at the same time he told it to me he said that it's only a rumor that Parlin is spreading around in order to beat her. I wouldn't put it past him. Parlin would be happy to spread the rumor. True or false, why should he care? If I didn't know what I know and I hadn't seen what I saw, I'd think it was a rumor myself. But at this point I wouldn't say anything about it. I just listen.

WHAT'S PAST IS PAST. I swore Pauline and Jeanette to silence about my little episode at Bayside. Nobody has to know. Why should it affect the election? Pauline told me there's a rumor that I'm in bad health. Nonsense. Except for that one day at Bayside, I'm in great health. All I have is poor circulation in my legs. But even that's OK. It just means that the hair on my legs has stopped growing and I don't have to shave them anymore.

What's past is past. But for some reason, maybe because Billy is going to get married soon, I keep thinking a lot about my own wedding. Such a beautiful affair, Ritz Plaza Halls, Passaic. I started wondering: Could the bandleader actually have been named Billy? Or was my memory playing tricks on me? Daymoor Billy would probably have been much too young to have been there, but the more I thought about it, the more possible it seemed. I remember insisting to my mother that we hire a young bandleader so he'd be sure to know the latest tunes. I kept thinking about it, and finally I decided: He may actually have been the bandleader who played at my wedding.

I went to the big dresser in the bedroom, Jack's side, and I dug my old scrapbook out of the bottom drawer. It was silly for me to look at it — let sleeping dogs lie, I always say — but I was curious, and there was a newspaper report about the wedding pasted in the scrapbook. When I found it, I saw that it gave all the information anybody could ever want about my bridal bouquet — stephanotis and lilies of the valley. It reported all about the wedding dress and veil, Alençon lace, really lovely. It gave the names of all my bridesmaids and ushers. But it didn't mention the bandleader.

Billy Symmes: I don't know why but I became certain. It was him. He was handsome, I do remember that; and when he put his clarinet — it was a clarinet, I swear it, I'd take an oath on it — next to his lips and played "Roses Are Blooming in Picardy" just for me, I broke away from whoever I was dancing with at the moment — it must have been Jack, only Jack, nobody but Jack in all those years — and I went over to the bandleader and I curtsied a thank-you; and he bowed and he took my hand and kissed it. Everybody applauded, even Jack. It was such a sweet scene. It must have been Daymoor Billy. Who else could be so suave?

W HEN I RANG ROSE'S DOORBELL to return the hat she left in my car, she sure was surprised to see me. But she's a gal who's always on the ball; she got on top of the situation fast. She swooped her arm like the royal usher and said, "Come right in. I'm honored."

"I've been looking all over for it," she said when she spotted her hat in my hand.

I couldn't pick up and leave just like that then and there, so when she invited me in for a drink I said yes, but not a serious drink because I'm not much of a drinker anyway.

I walk in and I put her hat on the table and I sit down and all the time she's staring at me. Finally she apologizes for staring. It was because I look so familiar to her. "Did you ever play at an affair in New Jersey?" she wanted to know. Never out of state, I told her, except in Providence, but there only a couple of times because it was so hard driving back to Boston late at night after an affair.

She brought out some fancy wineglasses and some ice and a can of Diet Pepsi, which is OK with me. Diet or fattening, I don't care. I was sitting on the sofa. She sat herself down right next to me and made a toast: "Happy days." So I toasted. She apologized because it was Pepsi not wine. She did have a bottle of champagne in the closet, she said, and she offered to put it in the freezer for a few minutes to chill. I told her to save it for her election day, when she had something to celebrate.

"I've got something to celebrate right now," she said. "I'm sitting on the sofa with a boy." And then she raised her wineglass so that I'd clink glasses with her again. What could I do? I clinked. Did she expect me to start trying to neck with her? She's not somebody who turns me on. But maybe she once was.

"Pretty racy, right?" I said, playing along a bit.

That must have embarrassed her because she changed the subject. "What note was that when the glasses clinked?" she wanted to know.

I told her I didn't know. If I had to listen that way to every sound I heard, it would drive me crazy.

"Well, let's clink again," she said. "And this time listen. I'm always happy to drive a man crazy."

When bait like that comes toward me, I have to bite at it. "I'm always happy to be driven crazy," I told her.

"I hope I haven't lost my touch," she said. Her answer almost knocked me off the sofa.

"Rose," I said, "I didn't know you were such a speedy gal."

That sobered her up. Her face changed color. She actually blushed. "Who am I kidding?" she said. "In my dreams I'm speedy, but in real life it's too late."

"Whoa. Don't say that," I told her. "It's never too late."

"If it's not too late for you," she said, "then it's too late for me." You had to hand it to her. She was right about that. So I stood up. It was getting time to leave anyway. She put her arms up to hug me good-bye, but then she put them down again.

"Don't worry," I told her. "I won't attack you." I headed toward the door.

She came after me. "I think we should kiss good-bye at the door," she said. What was I supposed to do, say no? Lips that touch Diet Pepsi will never touch mine? I don't know how she managed it, but she was right there at the door beside me. When she wants to be, she is a speedy gal, and she put her arms up for a kiss. I was going to kiss her on the lips. What the hell. If you're going to kiss, you kiss. But at the last minute she moved her face to the side, and all I got to kiss was a cheek. It was all dry and gray, an old lady's cheek. I felt like I was kissing my grandmother. I sure was glad to get back to Joyce.

IT TOOK ME A LONG TIME to get to see Dr. Polsky. Partly, it was my own fault. I kept postponing calling him. When I finally did get around to calling, his line was always busy and I had to press my redial button five or six times before I got through. Then I was told that the next available appointment was five weeks away. When I finally got to his office, the waiting room was so crowded that I had to sit reading a movie magazine for almost two hours before my turn came around. "Albert," the receptionist called out and then "Walter" and then "Sophie," as if Dr. Polsky's patients — every one of them elderly — were still kids in school. Finally she got around to calling out "Rose." Then I had to go into another room to wait again.

The only thing to read here were diplomas on the wall. I had plenty of time to read them and rehearse the question I wanted to ask Polsky when he finally got to me: If I'm having blackouts from time to time, hasn't modern medicine developed some sort of little machine to hook up to me and wake me up when it's happening?

Instead of answering, Dr. Polsky asked me a question of his own: Do I live alone?

Sad but true, I told him.

What he would like, he said, was for all the widows to double up and share their apartments with each other. Not me, I told him. I like my own house and I don't want anybody else in it, except maybe a new husband. Once I made that clear to him, he took out his stethoscope and started examining me. When he finished, he told me that they did have the kind of machine I was inquiring about.

Are you talking about something like a pacemaker, I asked him. They put it in and it regulates your heartbeat so there's no chance at all of your blacking out?

"Exactly," he said, and then he said something that made me want to wallop him: "But it doesn't come equipped with an alarm clock to buzz you and wake you if you do happen to fall asleep."

I didn't dignify that with an answer. They must think their patients are real dummies. Smart enough to pay the bills but then their brainpower runs down. But I did tell him I was worried about his putting a pacemaker into me because I didn't want him to leave a mark that was visible every time I came out of my house wearing a bathing suit. That's something I'd be very embarrassed about. One of the girls in my exercise class had some nodes taken out from under her arm after she had a lumpectomy on her breast. The lumpectomy doesn't show on her, but you can see scars from the operation she had under her arm. "I don't mind," she says. "I'm lucky to be alive. Why should I care about a few scars?" I'm sure she's right, but I still don't want anything to show.

"You're not planning to go swimming topless, are you?" he asked me. Some sense of humor! But then he assured me that after the pacemaker got installed, nothing would show even in a bathing suit. They tuck it in, right above the bosom. I'll still have to buy a new bathing suit though, something with a different cut.

But it was too soon to give me a pacemaker. I'd have to check into the hospital first for observation, he said, and then he'd see about it. Just for observation, he said, but the sooner the better. This week.

That means I'm going to have to miss the election.

Who's ever going to vote for me if I'm in the hospital? Nobody. They'll all learn about it. That sort of news travels like wildfire.

I DON'T THINK I'm in danger of kicking the bucket, she said while I'm driving her to the hospital. Joyce almost shouted at her. "Kicking the bucket! Stop talking like that, Rose. You mustn't think that way."

Joyce is right. Once you start thinking like that, you're getting ready to check out.

"Don't worry about the election tomorrow, Rose," I told her. "I'll put in an absentee ballot in your name."

"Don't bother with it," she said. "What's gone is gone."

I told her to stop thinking like that. You're in a battle, you stay in it until the bitter end. But she's right. It's all over. As soon as the news gets out about her being in the hospital, and especially when they hear why she's there, she can kiss her election good-bye. I wouldn't tell her, but I'm not even going to vote for her myself. That's all we need — another condo president popping off. It would be too demoralizing for everybody, especially for my buddies down at the pool. I can tell: Already some of them are counting how many days they've got left, and they don't like the numbers they come up with.

But I don't let that kind of thing affect me.

"Is anybody from your family coming down to see you in the hospital?" I asked her.

It turns out, she never even told anybody she was going in. She's got a daughter and a couple of grandchildren back up north, and she's got a sister; but she didn't say anything to any one of them. "What if your daughter telephones and she can't reach you?" Joyce said. "Don't you think she'd be worried?"

No problem, Rose tells her. The daughter only calls on Saturday — weekend rates. "By Saturday," Rose said, "I'll be home to answer the phone."

Joyce looks at me, and she taps me on the leg. I look at her too, sideways. Is this woman losing her marbles?

"Well, I'd call," Joyce says. "I think you should call them."

No answer comes out of Rose. It's like there's nobody sitting in the backseat.

If conversation about the election isn't going to distract

her and if her own kid doesn't interest her, what the hell would? I caught sight of her in my rearview mirror. "Hey, Rose," I said. "I see you're wearing the same hat you were wearing when we went to Bayside. Pink straw."

That pulled a smile out of her. "Since you brought it back to me," she said, "I've considered it my lucky hat."

"Keep wearing it," I told her. "Maybe you'll find a boyfriend in the hospital." That made Joyce slap my leg to tell me to shut up. But I knew what I was doing. "That's something that would cheer you up plenty," I said. "If it got serious, it would even make you call your daughter."

"You're letting yourself get carried away," Rose said. But she was smiling. I could see that. "The boyfriend part would be enough. It wouldn't even have to get serious." I squeezed Joyce's leg to tell her: See, I was right.

"I don't mind getting carried away," I said to Rose. "Let me enjoy myself."

But when we got to the hospital, she wouldn't let us stick around while she got herself settled into a room. "We don't mind waiting," I told her. "What else do we have to do with our time?" But getting her into her room would take them at least an hour, she said, and she was probably right. So we left.

It wasn't until we got back home that I discovered she left her hat on the car seat again. Maybe she left it there on purpose.

THEY PUT ME INTO A ROOM ALL BY MYSELF, which was fine with me because then I could take the bed by the window. The only problem was that the window looked out onto nothing. All I could see was a blank wall, another wing of the hospital, I guess. They brought me hospital food: mashed potatoes, canned peas, chicken with gravy, red Jell-o; and they brought a menu for me to circle what I wanted to eat the next day. I could order the same thing all over again if I wanted. The room was so air-conditioned that if you weren't careful, you could catch your death of a cold right there in the hospital.

After a while a nurse came in wheeling a big silver machine with a baby Christmas tree standing on it. "Are you Rose?" she asked me. I'm old enough to be her grandmother, but that made no difference to her. She still called me by my first name. When I admitted to being Rose, she said something that really infuriated me. "I want to introduce you," she said, "to your new boyfriend. He's a robot."

The machine had wires hanging down. There were little black windows on it and all kinds of knobs and dials. "You'll love being hooked up to him," she said. "He's a nice fellow. He'll be paying close attention to you all night." She must have caught sight of the look on my face, because she stopped short. "I'll be back later," she said, "to hook him up to you."

My robot boyfriend was going to watch over me while I was asleep. He'd count every breath I took. He'd listen to my heart beating. Joyce would be sleeping with Billy. Millions of other women, not just blonds, would be sleeping with men. Who would I be sleeping with? A machine.

At nine o'clock, the nurse came back. She had a tube of robot jelly in her hand. She squeezed out some of it and rubbed it on my temples. She was getting me ready for my new boyfriend. She squeezed some out and rubbed it on my arms and legs and on my chest right over the heart. I lay there still as a corpse. I felt like crying. Then she took some of the robot's fingers and ran them back and forth over my skin. She set them in place on top of every place where she'd put the robot jelly. "Try not to move," she said.

Who can fall asleep without moving around a bit? Not me. "I'll never be able to go to sleep like this," I told her. But she turned the robot on. "Once you're hooked up, I can't give you a sleeping pill. Beddy-bye," she said. "Night, night!" and she walked out of the room, leaving me there with my robot boyfriend.

He kept winking at me. I could see a green line moving around inside one of his windows. If this was a boyfriend, he was very attentive. He responded every time my heart beat. Sometimes he got so excited that his green neon line started flickering and lurching up and down.

No wonder he got excited. He was embracing me. His wires were wrapped around me. It wasn't a tight hug, but

still it was a hug I could feel. I was supposed to go to bed
with him. I was supposed to be comfortable enough to
fall asleep with him. I wanted to rip his wires off. I wanted
to get out of the hospital bed and start running. I was too
old to run away. Too old, that was the problem. I'm wearing out, my heart is wearing out, it hasn't been used
enough lately, use it or lose it, that's what they say, I was
losing it, not to anybody I cared about, only to a robot, a
machine. Where do I go next? To the presidency of the
Marilyn Circle Condo Association? I could forget about
that. Thinking such thoughts was no way to fall asleep.
They were going to keep me up; they were as bad as robot
light. I closed my eyes.

After I don't know how many minutes, I heard foot-
steps in the corridor outside my room. But nobody came
in. I was being left in privacy with my boyfriend.

Finally I must have dozed off.

But then, after a while, I heard somebody calling me.
"Rosie, Rosie!"

It was the voice of my father. He was the only one who
ever called me Rosie. I hadn't heard the sound of his voice
since he died in 1956.

"Rosie, Rosie!"

That was him, that was his voice. "Rosie!" he called out
to me. "Rosie!"

That's exactly what I heard him say.

"Rosie!" he called. "Rosie! I miss seeing you here."

[III]

Billy and Joyce

.

BAD PENNIES — they always come back. After the one night when I was sleeping alone, I hear my doorbell ringing, 9:30 A.M., and I go over to answer it and who's there? Roy, and he's not alone. "This is my friend Dennis," he says. No last name, no explanation, just Dennis. He doesn't even wait for a come on in. He's got his foot on the doorstep and Dennis is right behind him and I figure I'd better get out of the way before I get knocked over, so I step aside and slam bang they're both inside. "Your mother didn't tell me you're in town," I say to Roy.

"She doesn't know I'm here," Roy answers, and as he's saying it, it makes Dennis smile.

Dennis is a burly, bald guy with a big, pale face. You can tell he used to have a very bad complexion, acne, and he still has a pimple on his chin with a dark hair growing out of it. He's so ugly, he makes Roy look like Tyrone Power. Roy points at Dennis. "I told you about him. He's the expert on condo conversion."

"That's right," Dennis says. "When I go in there, you get your ten, fifteen percent plus, because after I get to them they're not going to buy at insider prices. But you got to move fast, because there's talk Boston's going to close down on conversion. They're making lots of noise about that."

"I worked up some figures for you," Roy says, and he waves a sheaf of paper in front of me.

"Is that the prenuptial?" I ask him. Without missing a beat, he says, "My brother is still looking at that in New York."

"Well," I say to him, "you tell your brother this: His mother's wedding ain't going to go ahead without the prenuptial. He's giving her a lot of grief."

"I promise you," Roy says. "When's the wedding? Six, eight weeks? I guarantee you'll have it your hands very soon. But I want to give you this today." He holds up his papers.

"Forget it," I tell him. "I don't want to look at it. Maybe," I slowed down. "Maybe just maybe, I'll look at it for you after I see the prenuptial. But I've got to have the prenuptial in my hand first. And then maybe I'll listen to your condo pitch." I looked his friend right in the eye. "That's a maybe. It's not a yes, just a maybe. Get it?"

"I'll be back," the heavy says. "I'll be back fast."

It left me with a bad taste in my mouth. I think I won't even mention it to Joyce. Let her kid tell her if he wants to.

I WON'T SAY I was the belle of the ball at the installation, but I certainly got my share of compliments. Part of the credit for it has to go to what I was wearing, my flame with the spaghetti straps; it comes with a little jacket, but I took it off after a while because in Florida you don't need it. People always like that outfit. I was worried about having nobody to dance with because Billy was up there leading the band. But I didn't really have anything to worry about. The only time I turned down a dance was after he dedicated a number to me, "Green Eyes." Even so, that Al Spear asked me to dance it with him — "You got green eyes," he said — but I told him I'd rather sit this one out since the song was dedicated to me. "All the more reason you should dance it," he said. But I didn't. I remained faithful to Billy. I was even wearing his topaz ring, though it doesn't really go with the flame.

It was a beautiful affair. Parlin's wife must have given him a talking-to, because he wasn't smoking his cigar. I am sorry Rose lost her election. My heart ached for her, but at least we didn't have to have a potluck installation. It was a regular affair, buffet, nicely catered. Rose couldn't be there anyway; she was just out of the hospital. I think her health is still bad, even with her pacemaker.

The treasurer was the only officer left over from last time, so he installed Parlin as president and then Parlin installed the new treasurer, who happened to be the old

one reelected. Then Parlin announced that he was form-
ing a new committee to keep up with the other buildings
in the complex to screen new purchasers and make sure
they fit into the Marilyn Circle lifestyle. What that means
is white, Billy says, but I think he's wrong. It's a mistake to
let in people who can't afford to pay the condo fees, because things could get run-down. I'd hate to see that happen; the plantings are so beautiful. Every time I see one of
those big cut-leaf philodendrons with a leaf that's turning
brown, my heart goes into my mouth. I hate it. Billy says
it's part of the natural process, but he's never taken care of
houseplants the way I have. Actually, it was Floie who
took care of the plants in my house, but it makes no difference.

I felt bad that I couldn't eat with Billy, because he was
playing music all the time while people were eating. I
went over to the buffet and brought him a plate, but it
was wasted; he wouldn't eat while he was playing. He
could aspirate something, he told me, and then he'd
choke to death.

Benny goodman in Moscow. Benny Goodman at
Carnegie Hall. Benny Goodman this. Benny Goodman
that. I don't have anything against Benny Goodman, I always liked him, he did a lot for the clarinet. But let's hear
it for Artie Shaw. He was really one of the greats. I always

loved Artie Shaw. I said that to Joyce the other day. "Who?" she said. "I never heard of him."

"You never heard of Artie Shaw!" I said. "I can't believe it. Where've you been?"

She looked kind of miffed. These haven't been such happy days lately. I know she's worried because her son's mixing into my business and she knows I'm not going to stand for it. "Artie Shaw the bandleader." I had to explain it to her. But that wasn't ringing any bells either. "He played the clarinet."

"Oh," she says, "Arrrtie Shaw. The one who was married to what's-her-name. Sometimes I don't understand you because of your Boston accent. Of course I remember Arrrtie Shaw. Once Monroe and I went dancing and he was playing."

"Lana Turner," I told her. "Artie Shaw married Lana Turner."

Monroe used to take Joyce out dancing all the time. I like to dance. When I invited her out dancing a couple of times, I got no for an answer. "Let's just sit home," she said. "I'd just as soon watch TV." So after a while I stopped even suggesting it.

As soon as that old biddy Rose started feeling better, she got her hooks into Billy to start up with the expeditions again. Into the Everglades to look at alligators, down to the Seminole reservation to play bingo. Alligators. If I want to see nature, all I have to do is turn on my TV; there's plenty of nature there, alligators, giraffes, pandas, anything you want. Yesterday they had a show about a bird called the yellow mudthrush. I watched it for a little while. Where do they get these animals? If I didn't see them right before my eyes on the TV screen, I'd think that they make them up.

Oh, the bingo! They have all kinds of people there — black, white, Cuban. They come down in buses from the South, from Alabama, Georgia, from Jacksonville — God knows where, all these southerners — awful. All washed-out-looking blonds, overweight. It's almost enough to make me ashamed to be a blond. I don't have to go out of my way to mix with people like that. I could see them on TV too if I wanted. They're the ones on *The Hallelujah Hour.*

It was so crowded we didn't even get four seats together. Rose had to sit next to this sweaty-looking farmer type, a real redneck, all polyester, a shiny blue polka-dot shirt. She didn't seem to mind. Poor Rose. Maybe it serves her right, the way they hatch up ideas for these expeditions at the pool. Billy's always ready to go along. What could make him happier? Driving along with a car full of girls. So I have to go along too.

Bingo wasn't any fun for Joyce, I could tell. Everybody else had a good time except for her. Even Rose, right out of the hospital. She loved it. She won twenty-four dollars, that helped. But Joyce, she had trouble working the squeeze-it grease pencil they give you to mark up your card. They don't give you little discs anymore. I guess people steal them. And then she got some of the grease pencil on her skirt. That stuff doesn't come off. "It's nothing," she said. "Never mind. Forget it. It's an old skirt, I've had it for ages. Its number was up." The skirt didn't look old to me. Everything Joyce wears always looks brand-new. You've got to hand it to her for that. She always looks like she stepped right out of an ad, I guess because her husband was in a branch of the women's fashion business.

And then she had trouble hearing the numbers, maybe because her hearing's going and there was so much background noise in the place. Chairs scraping, people talking to themselves, chitchat, that sort of thing. "B-fifteen," she cries out one time. "Did he or didn't he call B-fifteen because I have it." But nobody paid any attention to her. Everybody was too busy watching their own cards to answer her. They're fanatics there. They buy five, six cards at a time. Even I couldn't answer her. Unless I have a number myself, it flies right out of my head as soon as it's called. "B-fifteen," she kept saying. "B-fifteen." Not whispering it either. It made it hard for other people to concentrate on the numbers that really were being called. Finally I put her out of her misery. "No," I told her. "He didn't call B-fifteen." That very moment he called out C-twelve — I remember because I had that number and I squeezed my grease pencil to mark it — and over at the next table Rose stands up and screams, "Bingo! C-twelve. I got it! Bingo!"

If you're going to do it, I said to Billy, then for God's sake get in under the wire. Roy is calling me from New York; once he called me from Boston. Tell your friend he'd better move his ass — that's the way he talks to his own mother, move his ass. They're closing in, the renters, so no more apartments can turn into condos, he'll be up shit's creek. Shit's creek! Don't use that language with me, Roy, I told him. You should have more respect. You didn't learn that kind of thing at home. Not from Monroe, he didn't. Monroe was always a gentleman, in front of ladies anyway. Outside the home, I can't testify.

When I broached the subject to Billy, he said, "I don't want to get in under the wire." Roy had sent him up a paper to sign for the condo conversion, but he hasn't signed it. "I'm not signing it so fast," he said. "When I see the prenuptial signed, then maybe I'll decide to go ahead." And then he goes out onto the balcony with his clarinet and he starts playing. He looks funny when he plays the clarinet. At least his cheeks don't get puffed out like a trumpet player's. I couldn't stand that, even in a younger man. But he looks funny anyway. How can I tell him that? He'd be so hurt. So I arrange to sit myself in another room whenever he plays, and it sounds beautiful. It just doesn't look beautiful. I remember when my son Robert played the trumpet, his cheeks used to puff out. In a child that's cute. But not in an old man.

So he's out on the balcony playing a song. Guess what song. "Home, Sweet Home" by John Howard Payne. That's not the kind of song I ever heard any bandleader play before. He must have learned it in grammar school like I did. I have to admit it, it sounded pretty. But it was driving me crazy. He wasn't playing it for me. He was playing it for his tenants, the ones who might get evicted when his building gets turned into condos. He knew it and I knew it. I had to go out there and ask him to stop.

BE IT EVER so humble. I get out on the balcony and I start playing "Home, Sweet Home." It's a good thing it's winter; otherwise all the old ladies who heard it would start packing to head back to Times Square. I just stuck with that phrase — Be it ever so humble — and I played around with it. I changed the key, I speeded it up. I

slowed it down, I worked variations on the "Be it ever,"
and so on. And finally it must have got on Joyce's nerves,
she's edgy about no condo, because her son keeps getting
at her, so why should she take it out on me, he's not my
son, not yet anyway. Pleasures and palaces. I don't need
that, even if Joyce does. Pleasures OK, palaces, no. Then
finally she comes out on the balcony. I'm playing very
softly — and she says as nice as can be. "Can you stop
playing? I'm getting a headache."

I don't know what the connection is, but it made me
think about the guy who added "dooby dooby" to the
song about coffee and tea. Dooby dooby. That was his
contribution to the world. Maybe that and nothing else.
Maybe that's what he thought about when his time came:
millions of people singing "Dooby dooby." That's not so
bad; it could be worse. And then when he saw the light
flashing at the end — they say that's what happens when
you're going out, a light flashes — he heard a deep voice
from heaven calling out: Dooby! Then he heard it calling
out again: Dooby! And then an angel came down and
picked him up and carried him off to heaven. That must
have been how it happened.

I never made a million people sing "Dooby, dooby."
But I made hundreds of people, probably thousands of
them, cuddle and dance to "Paper Moon." That's an ac-
complishment, that's something I can be proud of. If I'm
not proud of it, at least I don't have to be ashamed of it.

So what if I never made the kind of money Monroe made? Did he really have anything to be proud of?

In my later years — I can't say in my old age, I'm not there yet — in the second half of my life, I've come to appreciate time more. They say that comes with maturity. It's my opinion that it comes from having digital clocks. I wake up sometimes in the middle of the night and what do I see? A magic moment. 1:11. 1:23. Sometimes 2:34. Usually it's a time that doesn't mean anything, 2:57 or 3:28. But when it turns out to be special — and there are lots of special ones, 3:33, 3:21 — I really love it. That's what they mean when they say you should appreciate the moment. Now I appreciate moments, minutes actually. It didn't used to be that way when they had regular clocks and watches with faces and hands, like little people.

I notice that sort of thing.

It used to be that if someone asked you what time is it and you looked at the clock, you'd tell them "quarter of eleven" or "almost four-thirty" or something like that. Now you tell them 10:46 or 4:28. "Quarter of eleven" is disappearing from the English language. Nobody says it anymore. Even if someone should happen to inquire about the time at that moment exactly, they never get told quarter of eleven. They get told 10:45. I don't even know if my grandchildren have learned how to tell time correctly.

They changed everything: Washington's Birthday, Columbus Day. It's not the way it was when I was a kid. The first day of spring used to be on the twenty-first of March. Then all of a sudden, it was on the twentieth. The same with the voting age. It was twenty-one. But then they moved it to eighteen. When people get older that's the kind of thing they complain about.

But there are plenty of good developments too. It's not all complaints. They walked on the moon. I saw them on TV. Television. Every once in a while when I'm looking at it, I get amazed: I'm watching Technicolor right in my own house. It's almost worth growing old for. When I grow old, I'm going to make the best of it. I know an old lady here in Daymoor, eighty-three years old, Louise, and she looks her age. But she doesn't care. "All the other women get up in the morning and look in the bathroom mirror," she once said to me, "and they're so disgusted by what they see that as soon as they catch sight of themselves they say: Yecch. I'm not like that. At this age I'm lucky to be here. I look in the mirror and I say: Good morning. How nice to see you again today. What a pleasant surprise." I hope I'm like that when I get to be an old lady.

Lorraine, this old friend of Alice's, called me up long distance and she kept asking me all these questions: Haven't I been your neighbor in the building for thirty years? Wasn't I one of Alice's best friends? Haven't I been a good tenant? And it was true, all of it, thirty years from her point of view, though you have to subtract a little from thirty because I moved down here four years ago. And now, she tells me, they're selling drugs in the hallways, cocaine, that's the story floating around. Alice must be turning over in her grave! More than once people called the cops into the building and the cops came and she'd love to move out like the Diamonds did and like the Pollocks. Do I remember the Pollocks? That's what she asked me? "Sure I remember the Pollocks," I said. "He had a luggage and leather goods shop." She wants to move out herself, somewhere safer, but where could she find a place now with everything so expensive?

Sit tight, I tell her. Don't make a move. I'll get the place straightened out. It'll be just the way it used to be when Alice was alive.

I sounded plenty calm while I was talking to Lorraine, but as soon as I hung up, I almost hit the ceiling. Cocaine! I can't remember the day when I was so pissed off. It was easy to see what was going on there. Roy must have had his Mafia friends move in on the building to get rid of the tenants and make way for condo conversion. I'm still waiting to see the prenuptial, and I'm going to have to fly up to Boston just to see what the hell's going on there. "Joyce," I said while we were having dinner at her place, not something she cooked, she seems to be slowing down on the cooking front lately, just something she ordered in, Chinese, she knows I like Chinese. I think that was her reason, anyway I hope it was her reason. "Joyce," I said. "I'm out of here."

When she heard that, she jumped up from her chair. I think she's nervous because we haven't got the prenuptial yet. "What do you mean, you're out of here?" she said. "What is that supposed to mean exactly?"

Maybe I should have found a more tactful way of putting it. But in a situation like the one I'm in it's hard to be tactful.

"I'm out of here," I told her, "means that in the middle of the winter I have to interrupt my life to go fly up to Boston to clean up the mess your son Roy's been making in my building."

"What are you talking about?" she asks me.

She wasn't putting me on. She really didn't know what I was talking about. So I told her. I told her how Roy started bringing in his Mafia buddies to clear all the tenants out of the building. "It's not a pretty picture," I said. "I'm going to have to kick your son's butt if he doesn't call off his pals. I'm going to have to get the cops in there. As it is, the cops have paid some visits to the building already."

"My Roy would never do anything that wasn't on the up and up," Joyce says. "Roy wouldn't do anything like that. None of my boys would. It's not in their nature." She was still standing up. She looked me straight in the eye, and it wasn't love light I saw shining there. "Furthermore," she said, "I resent your implying that Roy would do anything wrong." Then she sat down again.

I'm willing to share out blame. Her side, my side — what difference does it make? So I said, "Maybe my daughter-in-law is in cahoots with him." The more I thought about it, the more likely it seemed. Son of a bitch! My own daughter-in-law! Of course. She's the one who actually runs the building.

But Joyce wasn't having any of it. About her kid she's blind as a bat. "You never liked Roy," she said. "From the minute he came down here, I could tell." Well, that was no lie. She was right. I didn't like him. "And I was very pleasant to your daughter-in-law; and I treated your grandson so nicely though he's not an easy child — even you have to admit that." She stands up again and starts clearing dishes off the table. It was her good dishes we were using, not those paper cartons the Chinese restaurants send food over in. Nothing but the best for Joyce. Everything had to look perfect. Even the forks we ate with every day were sterling silver.

She's stacking up the dishes and she says, "What do you mean, you're going to kick Roy's butt? That's no way to talk to me! What do you mean you're going to call the po-

lice on him? How can you even think something like that?
I'm his mother. I'm your own fiancée." She sits down
again and pushes the plates away from in front of her.
"Why are you treating me like this? I never thought you'd
make me cry, Billy." She picked up one of her napkins —
Joyce never uses paper napkins on the table, only cloth —
and started holding it against her eyes. "You've always
been so much fun to be with, Billy. I always thought so.
But now that the chips are down, I guess I was wrong."

I'm not the kind of guy who weasels out of things. I
don't want to finger Roy. But I don't want to be taking the
blame either. "I'm not the one who's making you cry,
Joyce," I said. "It's your own kid making you cry. What's
he doing, sending the Mafia to sell drugs inside my building? Where the hell's the prenuptial? Who's got it? Roy
says his brother's got it, but it wouldn't surprise me to
learn that Roy's really got it himself and he's trying to get
hold of my building."

"Stop criticizing Roy like that! Stop it!" That's the first
time I ever heard Joyce raise her voice at me. I could see
tears on her cheeks. "Right now!" she said. She was really
crying. "Stop it! Don't you trust my family? If you don't
trust them, why should you care about the prenuptial?
Why should we even sign it?"

"That's up to you." That's exactly what I said. Joyce was
shocked to hear it. I have to admit it, so was I. "That's up
to you," I said again. When Joyce heard me say it, she set

the napkin she was holding down on the table and started smoothing it out. "How can we sign if it's not even here?" I said. "Don't get me wrong. Believe me, I want to sign. There's nothing I want more." When I said that, it made Joyce look a little happier. That is, she stopped crying. Then she began folding up the napkin.

Billy's the only real love affair I've ever had. I wasn't cut out for infidelity. I was always faithful to Monroe, except for only one time, maybe one and a half times. The one time was when I was in Paris while Monroe was off on one of his business trips to Frankfurt, West Germany. I was in this very fine restaurant, on the right bank, near my hotel, and there was a lovely, refined Frenchman eating his dinner out because his family was away in the country. A middle-aged man, very suave, like a Frenchman in the movies. He spoke English beautifully. We went up to his apartment. It was gorgeous. I'll say this: His wife had wonderful taste. But after that experience I decided I wasn't cut out for adultery. I didn't enjoy myself that much.

The only other time I ever even fooled around was with one of my neighbors from Flower Hill, Walter. He picked me up one day while I was walking to the train station and he offered me a ride into town. Naturally, I accepted;

I hate the train. A ride's so much nicer if the traffic's not bad. But traffic got stuck while we were going through the Queens-Midtown Tunnel. All we could do was wait it out. In the car right in front of us there was a couple smooching. "Look at that, will you," Walter said. Then as if on cue, we both turned around at the same time to look at the car behind us. Believe it or not, the same thing was going on there. I giggled. Walter put his arm around my shoulder, and I didn't take it away. In fact, I snuggled in toward him. He leaned over and kissed me and I kissed him back and then we kept right on kissing. I wouldn't let him do anything else. I kept my elbow in position so he couldn't get fresh. And as soon as the traffic started moving, we straightened up. "Well, that's it," Walter said, and he started driving again. And that was it. Whenever we saw each other again, we never made any reference to it, not even with our eyes.

W HEN I THINK of the winters, Boston, snow sticking to the trees, cars driving by so quietly you can hardly hear the traffic, even putting on the snow tires, even the chains when they used to have chains, I get a bit nostalgic. Marie used to love the winter best because that was when it felt so good to strip down in a warm room, which is something we never had the opportunity to enjoy, spending all our time together in that summer cottage. Joyce never would have understood it. "How can they live in houses like that?" she once said to me while we were driving over to Atlantic Boulevard and saw a street full of little cottages, black people, trailers, and so on. "How do they do it? I'd commit suicide if I had to live like that. I don't call it living." Joyce didn't spot the juicy little piece standing out in front of one of the shacks, just standing there, living. I could tell she had done some serious living last night, and she was going to do it again tonight. Oh, Marie! She knew how to live. Joyce knows how to live all right, but she keeps it separate from the rest of her life, like in a different compartment. I'm not like that.

I really wanted to give Marie a phone call when I was up in Boston checking on the building. Not just because I wanted her to help me get the hoods out of the building but because there was something about the weather that reminded me of her. No snow on the ground, just that chill; no sunshine, gray all day. All I kept thinking about was how we used to get together. I even looked her up in the phone book — her husband's name was Vito; they used to be in the North End — but nothing. Maybe she moved down the Cape, maybe she moved to Florida; but arrivederci, Marie. I couldn't find her. All she was to me now was a precious memory — how it lingers.

Mark and Jeffrey picked me up at the airport. Mark brought along a warm coat for me like I asked him to, and he put it over my shoulders as soon as he saw me. That way we didn't have to kiss hello like a father and son should. Mark never was a kisser anyway. All he did was pat my shoulder a couple of times. Actually, it wasn't a coat, it was a jacket, filled with down. Green. I never wore a green jacket before.

Driving to his house, we talked about the jacket. We talked about the Celtics. We talked about his new car, a Mercedes. We talked about Jeffrey's school. We talked about Jeffrey's bar-mitzvah, coming up. We talked about everything but what brought me up to Boston. Because the kid was in the car, I didn't want to mention the situation. I wouldn't be able to say anything without giving my opinion of how Margery was handling the building, and I didn't want to criticize her to her husband and her kid. Not that Mark was so eager to bring up the subject either. Who can blame him, caught between his wife and his old man?

I was going to mention something to him about it later that night after Jeffrey went to bed but, to tell the truth, I didn't have the heart to bring it up. Even thinking of talking to him about it, or to Margery, gave me a knot in the bottom of my chest, right over my stomach. I guess that's what it feels like when your heart sinks. It made my heart sink. My own flesh and blood turning against me like that, so I didn't say a word. Maybe the whole business made Mark feel the same way because he didn't say anything about it either. Margery too. It must have scared hell out of her because she kept her mouth shut. All she did was give me a kiss hello when I walked into the house. Plus she said, "When you go over to the apartment house, why don't you use my car?"

Mark leaves early to make his rounds at the hospital, and I took Margery's car and drove to Commonwealth Avenue to look over the building. She said she couldn't come with me because she said she had a dentist's appointment, she said. She's running the building. "What are you letting Roy's men in for?" I asked her while she was giving me my breakfast. "That's bad news. I'm going to bounce them out, that's why I'm up here."

"I gave Roy a free ticket to do whatever he thought was best to get the building ready for condoing. How could I know that this was what he was going to do?" How could I know? She knew. I'd bet my life on it. Roy told her there's a million dollars to be made, and her eyes must have lit up and she jumped in right behind him. "Don't rush me out of the picture," I told her. "Someday the building will be all yours and then you can play whatever games you want with it. But not yet. It's still mine."

When I drove up, the building looked run-down on the outside, but that's the nature of the game. Even while I was walking up to it, I could hear rock and roll, loud, out in the street. As soon as I opened up the outer door, it got a lot louder; and it got even louder when I opened up the door inside the lobby. That door wasn't even locked, a bad sign. So I locked it. All I had to do was follow the sound upstairs to the third floor. In 3-C, right next to the apartment I used to live in, the apartment where Alice dropped dead in fact, the door was open. The apartment was empty, but there was this radio in there turned on top volume. Apartment 3-C, Alice would have died all over again. I went in and shut off the radio and closed the apartment door, and I decided to go moseying around the hallways.

I didn't get very far before I heard that music coming at me again just as loud — not that I call that stuff music. I turned around and headed back to 3-C and this time there was somebody in the apartment — this thug, better looking than Roy's friend, sort of baby faced, a redheaded kid with a ponytail, but still a thug. Right away he challenges me. "You the guy who turned off my radio?"

"I'm the one," I said. "Don't put it on like that anymore."

"Who's going to stop me? I pay my rent. I got the right."

"Not anymore," I told him. "Your lease is up. You've been evicted." I looked at him to see if he had a gun in his pocket, but as they say in cop movies, he looked clean. Of course I wasn't in any position to frisk him to make absolutely sure. Even if I could frisk him to find out, I didn't really want to know. I didn't want to be in the same room with a gun.

"Who the hell are you?" he said, looking tougher by the minute. Big hands. Heavy work boots. He reached toward his pocket. He could be carrying a knife in there.

"I'm the padrone," I told him. "The godfather. I own the building and I want you the hell out of here." I was worried about touching his radio again, it might be dangerous, but I went over to it anyway and turned it off again. "You're history," I said.

"Hey, you son of a bitch, keep your hands off my property." I was standing between him and the radio, and his shoulders moved like he was going to push me. But before he could even raise his arms I sidestepped out of the way. "That's what I'm telling you," I said. "Hands off my property."

He reached into his right-hand pants pocket and left it there for a minute. I could almost see wheels turning inside his head. He was thinking it over: Should he cut me? Should he deck me? Should he just leave the premises and call it a day? " You son of a bitch," he said again, his shoulders twitching. "You son of a bitch."

That's when I knew I was going to come out of it safe, because when they talk, the don't hit. When they hit, they don't talk. You can see that any day on TV. Here's the proof: I'm still here to tell the tale. All he did was call me a son of a bitch again and stomp out of the room and stomp down the stairs. I could still hear him stomping as he slammed the lobby door behind him. Three-C is a front apartment. Out the living room window I could see him on the sidewalk, standing in front of the building. I had parked Margery's car right in front, a little Saab, cream colored with a five-number plate. It's an easy car to recognize. He knew that was the car I had come in and he went right up to it and kicked on the door. Then he kicked it again, a vicious kick, like he'd graduated from karate school. Thank God I was upstairs out of reach. I could have been on the receiving end of those kicks. Actually, Roy should have been there getting them.

Then he took something out of his pocket. Turns out he did have a knife after all. The edge of its blade must have been sharpened like a razor because he started running it up and down against the car door to make the paint come off. Five or six edge scrapes, very squeaky. I could hear them through the window, even though it was closed, January. It didn't take him long to make a real mess out of the door. I wasn't going to yell down to him: "Hey, cut it out!" With that knife in his hand he could run right back upstairs and cut part of me out. There was no phone in the apartment, no way for me to call the cops. He was working so fast the car would be junk by the time they finally got there anyway.

Then he moved on to the back of the car and tried to unscrew the license plate. That was risky. I wasn't the only person who could see him. Drivers passing by could see him too. But he couldn't get the plate off without a wrench or a pair of pliers, so all he did was twist it up-wards so it was practically folded in half. Strong hands. Thank God he didn't slug me. After he finished with the plate, he must have figured that was it, he'd done enough damage. So he went strolling off, heading down the street toward the trolley stop, not hurrying, not looking back. The trolley. He didn't even have a car with him. He came to work by public transportation. I guess the radio wasn't even his, just a piece of equipment he needed for the job, because he left it behind in the building.

Once he was out of sight, I went over to 4-H, to Lor-raine's apartment. Was she ever surprised! "I told you I'd come clean things up around here," I said. I never really looked much at Lorraine before. Why should I? She was a friend of Alice's. But she had fixed herself up a little, lost a few pounds. "My hero," she said to me. "I could kiss you. It was horrible. Worse than a slum. Like on TV, the inner city. It needed a lot of cleaning up."

She started telling me what they'd been doing in the building. They'd moved a couple of businesswomen into an apartment on the fourth floor. They had men coming up to visit them at all hours, night and day. The loud mu-sic was turned on all the time. The cocaine dealer was al-ways around waiting for customers in the lobby. "White?" I asked her. "Not always," was the answer.

When I got back to my son's house in that Saab, my daughter-in-law took one look at it and turned red in the face. "That's just a little message to you from your Mafia buddies," I told her. "Don't worry," I said. "The insurance will take care of it. Who have you got? Liberty Mutual?" That's who I've always had, and they've treated me very nicely.

She nodded yes. Liberty Mutual.

"Then all you have to do is tell them vandalism," I said. "But that's only half your problem. He said he's coming back. They don't give up so easily. So you station a cop at the front door. A cop in uniform. That'll keep undesirables away."

"How can I do that?" she said. Her voice was very small. No wonder. She screwed up, letting Roy take over. She should feel guilty. "They've already called the police down there several times," she said. She had a hell of a nerve playing with fire like that while my tenants are getting their fingers burned. Or maybe I'm the one getting burned. But not her. That's the way she was thinking. I could tell. I'm not going to put up with crap like that.

But now she's burned too. One look at the Saab showed her that.

"You got the Mafia in there, Margery," I told her. "Now it's your job to get them the hell out."

"That'll cost money," she said.

"Well then, you'll just have to pay for it," I said. "Not me. I don't pay. You. You pay."

"I'd have to take it out of the building rents." Her nose wrinkled. That idea smelled bad to her.

"No," I said very softly. "You can't do that. That cuts into my income, and I'm going to need every nickel that's coming to me." I gave the knife a twist. "Roy's mother is accustomed to the very best, and that's what I'm going to get for her on our honeymoon. The New Orleans Hilton. I'll send you a postcard. Maybe you can send it on to your friend Roy."

A room overlooking the Mississippi. Margery doesn't have to know that I get a twenty percent senior citizen discount. Joyce doesn't have to know it either. It's still expensive. Joyce will be living in the lap of luxury.

"Hire some off-duty cops," I told Margery. "Have them standing at the front door twenty-four hours a day, in uniform. Three eight-hour shifts. It's expensive, but it's the only thing that'll work. No cheating. No empty hours." I shook my finger at her. "I'll be watching. I have my spies."

"Wait till I die," I said. "But while I'm living I want it clean. And I'm going to live a long time."

"We won't be able to do anything but collect rents," my daughter-in-law said. "The era of condo conversions is coming to an end."

"Well," I tell her, "just do what I'm telling you to do. Maybe the era will come around again someday. But you'll have to wait."

And the next morning she drove me to the airport in that dented, scratched-up Saab, and I caught a plane back to Florida.

I HATE TO QUARREL with Billy. I hate to quarrel with anybody, but with Billy especially. But we kissed and made up when he got back from Boston — he was only gone for two days. The situation couldn't have been so terrible if he could fix it up that quickly. He didn't tell me about it and I didn't ask him about it and so everything was just the way it had been before, though I still had sort of a bad taste in my mouth.

But then I felt bad again when we got into bed that night. I hesitate to say anything to him about it, but sometimes I get scared when he's making love like a young man not like an old man; and then afterward he practically collapses on the bed beside me, he's so exhausted. I worry about him having a heart attack, you hear so many stories, even jokes you hear. I don't even have him yet and then I could lose him so easily. It almost tempts me not to get married because I wouldn't be a bride, I'd be a nurse. I get these awful premonitions. To have to go through with somebody else what I went through with Monroe, when he was bedridden, so weak he couldn't even peel a banana. I'd hate it, I couldn't take it.

I wouldn't be thinking this way except for the fact that he gets so pale when he's lying there trying to recover and catch his breath again. And then when that's done with he's as frisky as ever, full of energy, full of jokes, all kissy-kissy. He's practically ready to start all over again, but I won't let him, I won't have any of it. I'm too worried.

You'd think he'd notice, you'd think he'd be able to show some sensitivity to what I'm feeling. But forget it.

I GET HOME, I hear my doorbell ringing at 9:00 A.M. I go to open the door and it's like a bad dream come back all over again: There he is, Roy's buddy, Dennis. He pushes his way right inside the door like he's my buddy too.

"Did you think you weren't ever going to see me again?" he asks, and he closes my door behind him like it was his house, not mine. "After the way you treated my boy in Boston the other day, did you really think I was going to forget about you?"

How I remembered him was that he was homely and pudgy looking. Now I could see that there were muscles there. Not a man I was eager to tangle with. "Besides," he said. "Now you've given me a good reason to come down here to Florida. I ought to thank you."

I didn't say anything. I figured I'd let him talk.

"And here's how I'm going to show my appreciation," he said. "Just to prove that I'm not all bad, I brought down the paper you've been waiting for. I'm delivering it for Roy. I'm the delivery boy and I'm going to sit right here waiting while you sign it." He sat down on my sofa with the paper on his lap, and he pulled a pen out of his shirt pocket and held them both out for me to grab hold of.

I didn't take the paper. I didn't take the pen.

"What's the gimmick?" I pulled out one of the dining chairs so it was facing him, and I sat down on it. "What the hell do you want out of me anyway? If it's my building, forget it. You ain't going to get it."

"Just sign the paper," he said, and he wagged the pen at me. "Just hand me back the paper and I'm out of here fast."

"If Roy was here," I said, "I'd smash his face for him."

"Stop talking so tough. You don't have the muscle for it." And he flexed his arm to show me who did have the muscle. "Sign the paper," he said.

"First I show it to my lawyer."

"Your lawyer?" His voice squeaked. That was something I didn't remember about him. "It's already been to a lawyer, Roy sent it. Don't worry, it's on the up and up. You don't need to show it to no lawyer." He wiggled the pen at me again. "All you got to do is sign."

I went up to him and grabbed the paper. What harm could it do to read it? "You're going to give me a heart attack," I said.

"No problem. Then the building goes to your son."

I read the paper. If I signed it, I'd turn over control of the building to my daughter-in-law and my son. Not ownership, just control. "You're dreaming," I said.

"You get real cute when you're mad. Look at you," he said. He came up real close and stood right in front of me. I could smell him. His clothes hadn't been to the dry cleaner's in a long time. "Look at you," he said, and he put his fat fist right next to my chin, under it, close but not touching. I moved my head back but his arm followed me. I could hit him in the balls with my own fist, but I didn't dare try anything on him, he had me scared, I didn't want to start up with him. "Get the hell out of here," I said. "Get your ass out of here, and if you don't, I call security on you."

Not the cops, security. He could see where the phone was and cover it, but he had no way to tell where the security buzzer was.

"Security," he said. "Security for your old age. A million at least, but only after you condo."

" You get your ass out of here." I don't know how I got the strength to say it again. "Or you're in big trouble. That's all the security I want. And I'm going to get it if you don't move."

He leaned forward and snapped his fingers at the paper sitting on my lap. "Mail it to your daughter-in-law," he said. "If she don't have it by the end of the week, she's in trouble."

"She's in trouble already," I said. He didn't answer me. He didn't look at me. All he did was walk out the door.

FINALLY, FINALLY, the prenuptial has arrived. It must have been so difficult for the boys to do. It was Monroe's money and Monroe was their father. But I knew my boys would never let me down. Registered mail, $4.85 worth of stamps on it. The postman came all the way up to my door and I had to sign for it. Four copies, one for me, one for Billy, and two to send back to the lawyer. I thought: Should I call Billy and wait for him to get here and we can sign it together? That would be nice and romantic. Or should I sign first and then call him? That's the decision I made. By the time he got here I had all four of them signed.

"Well," he said when he came in the door and gave me his kiss. "At last. They sure cut it close. I almost thought they weren't ever going to get here." I didn't say anything because I don't like to hear my boys criticized. I just handed him a pen. But he wouldn't take it. "Aren't you going to sign it?" I said. "After all that wait? Why don't you sign it now and then we can forget all about it and never have to think about it again?"

But he wanted to take it home and read it at his leisure before signing it.

"Don't you trust my lawyer?" I said. "I'm sure it's all right."

"Maybe I'll have my own lawyer look at it," he told me. I didn't even know he had his own lawyer.

"How long is that going to take?" I asked him. "We finally got it and now you want to start another delay. Is it going to affect the wedding?" I shouldn't have said that. It was my team that held it up. But my nerves were getting on edge.

"You know me," Billy said. "I move fast."

It really made me feel bad. Here I've been on the spot for so long, and now that I'm finally off the spot, it turns out I'm still on it. "I'll put on something for lunch," I said. All I had the heart to do was open up a can of cold soup because I always keep some vichyssoise on hand, which is something I know he likes. But he didn't want it. "I think I'd better go home and read this thing over and then get it moving," he said. And he picked up the envelope with the four copies of the prenuptial in it and he gives me his kiss good-bye and presto, he's out the door. I could hardly get myself to kiss him back.

WITH MARIE I always used to feel like a king — varoom — there was no stopping me, I was that powerful. Like Zeus. Once I got started, I went into overdrive, it was something. Like it was a hurricane, like a force of nature, every time, every damn time. That was Marie. It's never been like that with Joyce, and that's not just because I'm older now. I wasn't a kid then, I was in my forties. But Marie worked something on me, maybe it was Italian, maybe it was some magic she knew about, passed down from Italy.

It's not like that with Joyce. Sure, I'm older now, but also I'm different. I wasn't kidding myself when I said I never had such a good time as I've been having with Joyce, even though it's been tapering off a little bit as time goes by and — I've got to admit it — as the wedding gets closer. But with Marie it wasn't about just having a good time, it was something else, it was like we were both of us being driven.

That was wonderful.

We'd been going at it for five, six years — at that cottage except for during the summer; and in my car during the summertime, parked in the woods near Walden Pond sometimes or up in the Blue Hills Reservation — I liked to vary it; it added a little kick when it was a new place, and it brought back memories whenever we did a reprise. Then in the car one day, after five or maybe even six years, I don't remember which, Marie lowered the boom on me. "After today," she said, "it's going to be good-bye."

"Have you got somebody else?" I didn't think so, but that was what came into my mind, that was all I could think of to say, I was so shocked.

"Just Vito," she said.

"Then why change things?" I put both of my hands on her. "What do you mean good-bye? Never again? You must have finally turned crazy." She always used to tell me I knew how to drive her crazy.

"Maybe I've finally sailed over the edge," she said.

That was no answer, I told her. Let me know your reasoning. Tell me why we're finished. I should say why *you're* finished," I said. "I'm not finished."

Finally she explained: One time when her period was late she started to worry. Was she pregnant? If she was, who was the father — Vito or me? Then two or three months running, her period was late again. She was beginning to worry: Was it time for her to go through the change?

"It's nothing," I told her. "You should see Alice. She's a real hot flasher."

Marie didn't think that was funny.

"I don't have hot flashes," she said. "But I'm starting to have funny feelings."

I didn't see why that should stop us.

She gave me her reason. It was a half-ass reason, but I believed her. "I don't really trust my diaphragm that much. Or those rubbers. If I'm going to be late on my period," she said, "or miss a month from time to time, I couldn't stand the tension, am I pregnant? I already had that before I got married. I don't want to go through it again."

Nothing I said could make her change her mind. "Well, that proves it," I told her. "I'm not so irresistible. All the times you said you couldn't resist me you were lying. Now you can hold out on me."

"Don't be wise-ass with me," she said. "I'm serious."

She found a way to show me again how I'm irresistible to her, but it was only for that afternoon. Still, I wasn't going to let her go so easy, just like that. I got her to agree to

one more time. I'd arrange it, I told her. A nice motel in
Worcester — nobody knew us in Worcester — and that's
where we had our final get-together. I was hoping it
would be fun, but it was no fun. We went at it, God
knows we went at it, but we both of us were too sad to really enjoy ourselves. She even cried. That was practically
the last I ever saw of her, sitting up in the motel bed, her
back against a pillow, sniffling. "I'm going to be a brave
soldier," she said, and she stopped herself from crying. I
didn't feel like a brave soldier myself, that's for sure. She
had left her car in Natick at a Stop & Shop on Route 9,
and I drove her back there and dropped her off. Oh,
Marie! Oh, Marie! Arrividerci means I'll see you again. I
couldn't even say arrividerci to her. Oh, Marie! That's all I
could say when we said good bye. No kiss. I just squeezed
her hand. "Oh, Marie," I said. "Oh Marie." And I kept
saying it and singing it all the way home in the car. I was
a real wild man that night. Alice must have thought I'd
gone crazy. But I didn't hear a word of complaint from
her.

Now I'm going to have to put Marie out of my mind.
Lois too, every one of them, plus anyone else who might
come up in the future. I'm a little sad about it, because
nobody likes to give up on himself, on the best part of
himself that is. But I got the prenuptial back from my
lawyer and he looked it over and he didn't find anything
wrong with it, sharp as he is. So now there's nothing

standing in the way of the wedding. Now she's really got me hooked.

Roy is right about one thing — though I'd never admit it to him: Billy doesn't know how to live the big-ticket life. Give him a couple of women to flirt with and he's happy. That's all he needs. Well, his flirting days are over as far as I'm concerned. I mean I don't mind my husband paying compliments to my friends — though how he can tell Rose that she's a hot number is beyond me. Rose. Her face lights up when he says it, and he has the bad taste to say it right in front of me, not only where I can hear him but when other people can too. I think she's sweet on him. If he thinks Rose is so great, the maybe he should marry her instead of me.

I've noticed: Sometimes Rose has trouble catching her breath. Maybe that doesn't mean too much. Even Billy gets short of breath from time to time. His health doesn't worry me so much as the flirting does and — I have to admit it — the fact that he doesn't know how to spend money. If he had his own way, we'd only eat out at restaurants that have early-bird specials. That way he misses a lot of good meals. There's a terrific restaurant in Deerfield Beach, La Cuisine, that has the most wonderful desserts. Their crème brûlée is out of this world. It reminds me of the first time I ever ate it, at that restaurant in Paris where I met Monsieur Handsome. It was wonderful there, and it's wonderful here too. But I can't get Billy to go there because he's reluctant to pay full price for a meal. Am I going to have to spend the rest of my life eating early-bird specials because Billy's so tight?

I volunteered to be the one to take him out to dinner, but he said, and I quote directly, "No, that's the man's job, to pick up the tab." OK. Let him pick it up, but at least let him show me a nice time, not take me out to some crummy restaurant, like the ones his pal Rose and her friends go to. I can't stand that.

I wouldn't mind, but if he'd turn his building into condos the way Roy suggested, he'd have money to burn.

WHEN I WAS on Commonwealth Avenue, in the building, making sure Roy's buddies got the hell out of there, you'd think I'd be remembering Alice. After all she was my wife, we lived there together for thirty-four years, she's the one who got me to buy the building, she figured it all out and saved up the money to pay for it. But it wasn't Alice I kept thinking about, it was Lois, my little pal on the second floor, the one I had something going with but only for a few months. She had moved out of the building, I knew that, in fact she left even before Alice died, while I was still living there. I was sorry to see her go even though it was all over, and I know she was sorry to see the last of me too. She moved out to Canton, maybe Randolph, one of those towns down there.

Her last name was Halpern, so I looked her up in the South Shore phone book, figuring maybe I could call her up and say hello just for old times' sake, just for sentimental reasons. I thought it would be nice to have a little reunion with her after all these years. But I was going to get married again and there weren't going to be any more reunions like that in the cards for me. I figured if I called her from the airport while I was on my way out of Boston, there'd be no danger of our really getting together. Well, there she was right in the phone book. Her husband's name was Billy too. All I had to do was dial her number, deposit twenty-five more cents please, and let it ring. And I got her.

"Billy," she screamed when I told her who it was on the phone. "Billy." And then she lowered her voice. "I'd love to see you again." She was whispering when she said that.

It was one of those wall phones they have in airports, no privacy, but if you know how you can make a conversation feel private even on one of those things. So I whispered myself. "I'd love to see you too," I told her. "I'd love it. I'd love it." Then I told her how much I'd been thinking about her, how much I wanted to get to her, how much I wanted to have a reunion.

"Let's do it," she said. "Tomorrow's Wednesday. I can go into Boston easily on Wednesdays. You tell me where and I'll meet you."

"Wednesday," I said. "Tomorrow. Wednesday I'll be a thousand miles away." Then I told her why I couldn't see her, I told her I was going to get married again, I told her it was all over for me now, playing around, I told her I telephoned because I wanted to have something sweet to remember, I told her I'd be thinking about her tomorrow, I told her I'd be thinking about her every Wednesday, I even told her I'd be thinking about her on my honeymoon.

That's the only time a woman ever hung up on me.

I don't know what made me call her up and talk to her like that, like I was a dirty old man getting my kicks just from talking about it. I don't have to do that kind of thing, God knows, and I hope I never do have to do it. Maybe I was doing it because Lois was young. That's the way I remember her anyway, that's the way she sounded over the phone, nothing changed from twenty-five, thirty years ago. And Joyce, I've got to admit it, Joyce is old.

Still, I never did anything like that before and I hope I never do it again. It wasn't the real me talking. That was a dirty old man act, she was right to hang up on me, I should have just hung up myself. What made me talk that way I don't know. Women always have an excuse for any crazy thing they happen to do: It's their period, and if it's not their period, it's their hormones. They've got a whole repertoire of excuses: menopause, the change, all that stuff. Maybe it was hormones with me too. Something got out of control. Men have hormones too. Blame it on testosterone, I've always had plenty of it. Maybe now it's running down. I've seen evidence of that, that's why, the testosterone is getting shaken up inside of me and it affected my behavior.

"WHO WAS that Spanish-looking girl I saw coming out of your condo this afternoon?" I said to Billy. It looked suspicious to me, a very attractive girl with access to his house, very attractive and too young to be a resident here.

"What Spanish-looking girl?" he said, so innocent you'd think butter wouldn't melt in his mouth. "What girl?"

"That's my question exactly," I said to him. "What girl is she?"

He didn't answer for a while. He looked puzzled. Maybe he was trying to think up an answer. "Oh!" he said as if the light was suddenly dawning on him. "Oh. Connie. I got her to come by and do some cleaning." What kind of cleaning? I didn't believe him. "Since I'm going to have to sell the place after we get married, I figured I'd better do what I can to keep it in good shape. So I called an agency and had her come in."

"Why didn't you ask me about it?" I said. "I could have

sent over my girl." Melba. I think she'd be safe with him. She's too fat and too black. "Melba," I said. "She always does a wonderful job."

He said he didn't want to bother me, and while he was talking, he looked me straight in the eye. "Does she do a good job?" I asked. "How much does she charge?" I didn't get an answer right away. If this girl was on the up and up, he'd tell me five or six dollars, maybe seven fifty because it's hard to get them. I pay Melba seven fifty, and she's worth every nickel of it.

"Minimum wage," he said, and I knew he was lying to me.

"That's disgusting." I was furious. If he wants to play games with professional girls, that's up to him, but then to come into my house and into my bed and pretend nothing like that happened is something I'm not going to put up with. "She wasn't a cleaning woman, Billy," I said. "She was some bimbo you got to come visit you."

I happened to be wearing the topaz ring he gave me. An awful color, an awful ring. I had half a mind to take it off my finger and throw it in his face. Maybe the bimbo would like it. But I restrained myself.

"What are you talking about?" he said. "What do you mean, a bimbo? You want to come over and inspect my apartment? Let me tell you, the laundry's all done, everything's been cleaned, the bathrooms, the refrigerator. Come on. I'll show you."

"Visit? The way I feel now," I said, "I don't ever want to set foot in there again."

"What the hell are you talking about?" he said to me. "What the hell do you mean?"

He knew damn well what I meant.

THE ONLY reason I had Connie come by to see me again was because I started thinking about Marie. No question about it: Joyce is tops, there's nobody like her; but Marie had a kind of wildness to her, maybe it was because we were doing something we weren't supposed to be doing, we were doing it on the QT, and that added an edge to things. Maybe that's what I was missing, the *musn't* part of it, the forbidden part. But then there was another thing. Joyce got tickets for the Fort Lauderdale Symphony Orchestra; they were having a concert and she figured it might be something I'd enjoy and she was right. It isn't like going to Symphony in Boston — I managed to do that maybe one time a year, maybe it was twice — but it was the equivalent, sort of. At least it's the best they can do around here.

So she got these tickets, and we got dressed up. I even wore a necktie and my new blue shirt, periwinkle blue Joyce calls it, she ought to know, she bought it for me, and I took her out to dinner at the seafood place she likes, full price, no early bird, and we went to the concert. We're sitting there listening, for a time I'm even holding her hand, but then after a while I let go of it because my own hand was getting sweaty, it was hot in there, maybe the air-conditioning wasn't turned high enough, that might be because they were worried it could interfere with the concert. They were doing the Mozart clarinet concerto. That's a piece I practically know by heart because I used to have a Mozart Minus One record of it and I used to play the clarinet part along with it.

Well they were playing the second movement, very slow and sweet, and all of a sudden I heard a funny, raspy little noise and I looked over at Joyce. It was coming from her. She was fast asleep with her mouth hanging open, and she was snoring. I wasn't the only one who could hear it. There was a couple sitting in front of us nudging each other and starting to turn around. I couldn't believe what I was hearing. Here we'd been sleeping together in the same bed for five, maybe six months, and I never heard her snore. Now, in the middle of a concert, is when she decides to snore.

I figured I better wake her up. But before I squeezed her arm to wake her up, I took a good look at her sitting there with her mouth open, and I thought: My God, she really is an old lady. As soon as I put pressure on her arm, she woke herself up so easy you couldn't even tell she was sleeping. No sudden movement, no little grunts, no yawn. She blinked a couple of times and stretched her shoulders and that was it, a very classy performance. But there's no denying it, she's an old lady.

I have to admit it, in that crowd Joyce wasn't the only one that fell asleep. There was this old guy sitting a couple of rows ahead of us and he was really snoring loud, like a sawmill, so bad that the lady sitting behind him had to tap him on the shoulder a couple of times before she could wake him up. He was an old man. Joyce was an old lady. That's why I called up Connie and asked her to come up and visit me a second time. And I didn't pay her any minimum wage either. I don't think Joyce swallowed that story. I've been sleeping in Joyce's bed, but that's all I've been doing there — sleeping.

IT'S HAPPENED. Just what Roy was afraid of. They passed a law in Boston clamping down on condo conversions. Now half the tenants have to vote in favor before any building can get converted. Roy called me up to tell me about it. "Inform your boyfriend," he said. "Inform your boyfriend that he's won his game." Then Roy laughed, his nasty laugh, angry. "Your boyfriend won," he said again. "Some victory. I don't call that winning. It means he lost. I'm out every nickel I spent on his building. Now he's out of luck with his conversion. It would

have been a million easy for him. A million. A million
two maybe. That's the way your boyfriend is taking care
of you. Nothing! Now he don't even have a pot to pee in."

That's Roy's way. When he's angry he talks as if he grew
up in a truck driver's household. I wouldn't say a word
about it to Billy. Why should I listen to him criticizing
Roy? Let him be smug if that's the way he wants to be.
He's still got his $26,000 a year from the rents. Twenty-six
thousand plus his $9,000 Social Security, and that's all he
needs according to him. Thirty-five, period. That's it.
Thirty-five. That's his income. No wonder he buys
topazes. It's a good thing I have my own money coming
in, or otherwise I'd be spending the rest of my life trying
to swallow those early-bird specials. And then trying to
digest them. I don't understand how people can live like
that, especially if they don't have to.

If Billy wants to spend his thirty-five a year on some
minimum-wage bimbo, that's up to him, but it's not anything I'm going to put up with. I know he's a man with
strong needs — I can certainly testify to that fact — but
that doesn't mean he's supposed to play around like that.
The diseases. Especially these days. And then to come
into bed with me. What Monroe chose to do during his
business hours wasn't really my concern until one day
when he came home and brought me his crabs. God
knows how people get such things. It was unforgivable. I
made him spend an entire year without touching me un-

til I finally did forgive him. Who he was touching in the meantime wasn't my concern. I didn't give a damn. Crabs! I made him go out to the drugstore and buy some medicine, some awful chemical, and I washed with it; and I made just as sure about the sheets and the towels. It was the same medicine I had to use the time Robert came home from fourth grade with nits. That sort of thing doesn't surprise you in the city. Kids get nits. But in Flower Hill you don't expect it. And when you're married you don't expect crabs either, not from your husband. God knows what that bimbo gave Billy. Minimum wage my foot. A cleaning woman. I bet she cleaned up on him. I'm letting Billy sleep in my bed, but I wouldn't let him come near me and he knows it, he hasn't even tried.

The invitations are all out and the wedding is in two weeks and maybe I made a big mistake. I'm not too proud to call it all off, even if I do have to listen to Roy telling me how dumb Billy was about his apartment house.

I T REALLY HIT the fan. She saw Concepción coming out of my condo and she put two and two together. She didn't believe me when I tried to explain it. At first she didn't say anything, but then after a couple of days went by, very quiet, she started asking me all these little questions, needling me. "How can you get such a nice-looking

young girl to clean for you at minimum wage?" she
wanted to know. That's who the agency sent, I told her.

"What's the name of the agency?" She kept asking me
questions in a funny little voice, like she knew it was all a
joke. "I don't remember," I told her. "I found it in the yellow pages," "Oh, really!" she said. "If I called them, do
you suppose they'd send somebody over to me at that
price?" "Sure," I said. "Why not?"

I kept playing along, figuring she'd have to drop it
sometime. But she went into the kitchen, and I heard her
opening up one of the kitchen cupboards — that's where
she keeps her phone books — and she came back into the
dining room, where I was sitting. She was carrying the
yellow pages, and she set it down on the table right in
front of me.

"What was the name of the agency?" she said. "I'll call
them up right now." I told her I didn't remember, so she
opened up the phone book and pushed it in front of me
and told me to look through all the listings to refresh my
memory. I felt like Reagan up before one of those Congress committees. I'm sorry but I have no recollection.
That's what I wanted to say. I plead the Fifth Amend-
ment. I looked all down the listings, and of course I
couldn't find it.

She pulled the phone book back toward herself and
started turning pages. "Maybe this will help your memory," she said, and she pushed the book back at me. She

had it all figured out. The page was open to "Escort Service."

"What are you talking about?" I said. Just for a second while I was saying it, unfortunately, I let a little smile show, I couldn't help it, it escaped out of me, and she spotted it because she was looking at me all the time to see my reaction.

"You know damn well what I'm talking about, you know what I mean, bringing a whore into your house and then having the gall to come and sleep in my bed afterwards as if nothing had ever happened, while your hands were still dirty from her. Your hands! I shouldn't say your hands. It's not your hands I should be talking about. You're disgusting, that's what I think, disgusting. You disgust me!" All the time she was saying this, more than this, she kept at it, twice as much, three times as much, she didn't raise her voice, she didn't shout; but the words kept coming at me, cold and fast like a blizzard. "I don't know what you're talking about," I said. "I don't know what you're saying."

"Here's what I'm saying," she said. "What I'm saying is that I'm not going to put up with that kind of thing. Ever! What I'm saying is that it's disgusting. What I'm saying is get out of my house." She stood up and pointed at the door. "I mean it," she said. "Get out! I mean it. I'm not kidding. Get out of this house!" She walked over to the door and opened it. "Right now," she said. "Get out right now!"

What was I going to do? Try to cool her down? It sure wasn't going to work to try to warm her up. "You got it all wrong," I said. "You're not being fair to me." But we both knew I was lying.

"I'm being fair to me," she said. "Get out!"

So I left.

H E DOESN'T KNOW what the word *love* means. That's exactly what I decided to tell him. Why not give it to him straight? Why should I pull any punches? To spare his feelings? What a laugh. But I couldn't say it until after I finished with the cancellations. That was a job and a half. All those phone calls. Heartbreaking.

First, I called up the Boca Chateau and I told them I had to cancel. "Is it really cancel?" they said. "Or is it postpone?" I guess they were trying to hold on to the business. "Cancel," I told them. "All over. Finished. Wiped out." That means I lost my twelve-hundred-dollar deposit. I called up the florist and cancelled my whole order: a variety of lilies, big ones and little ones all in different colors. It would have been beautiful. That didn't cost me anything. I called up the woman who did the invitations and told her to send out cancellation cards to everybody she had sent an invitation to. It turned out she still had the list of addresses from the invitations. She always keeps them for a couple of years, she told me, just in case; and also she sometimes gets a commission to do the thank-you notes. She even told me what wording to use on the notices. "Just don't say Joyce Tarlow regrets," I told her. "I don't regret." "Don't worry about it," she said. She's done it before. This wasn't the first wedding that's ever been canceled.

I cancelled the reservation for the restaurant dinner we were going to have the night before the wedding. I cancelled the hotel reservations for my sons and their families. I had one of my grandsons in the same room with Billy's grandson. I cancelled it. At the hotel I cancelled the tennis court reservations Robert's wife had asked me to make for her. There's only one person I didn't notify about the cancellation: Billy. He'll find out soon enough.

I waited until after I had spent the entire morning on the telephone cancelling before I let myself go. And then I cried. I didn't think I was going to cry that much, I'm not a crybaby. Even when Monroe died I didn't cry so much. When he finally died that was a relief to me because he'd been through so much. I cried a lot when my father died — not so much for my mother but for my father, yes. But Billy made me cry. I was sitting right on my sofa, but I got up and closed the door to my balcony because I didn't want anybody to hear me the way I was bawling. I went and got a towel out of the guest bathroom, not one of those ditsy little guest towels either, and I put it over

one of the yellow sofa pillows I have and I held the pillow
up against my face and I bawled. Finally I said to myself:
Why am I crying so much? It isn't as if somebody died.
Who died? I kept saying it out loud. Who died? because I
couldn't believe I was crying so much. Who died? The
more I said it the more I cried, the more tears kept coming out of my eyes. Who died? I'll tell you who died, I
died. Something inside of me died, it collapsed and died,
poof, gone, like a balloon.

But after a while I shut up. What was I going to do,
spend the rest of the day crying? Maybe the rest of my
life? I'd have to be crazy. The invitation lady was right,
this wasn't the first time a wedding was canceled. Usually,
they're younger when it happens though, they have a
whole lifetime ahead of them to recover. I'm sixty-seven.
But nobody has to know that. Even Billy never knew. Nobody's going to look up my birth certificate.

Besides, I'm a young sixty-seven.

I'M NOT GOING to admit to her that I screwed up, but
there's no question about it: I did. Not that I have to
worry about spending my sunset years all alone. I won't
have to do that. Every time I turn around there's a brand-
new widow available here, and they're not all old ladies
like her either. They've just arrived at Daymoor and

they're happy to make my acquaintance. Whatever I want, it doesn't matter. But Joyce was something else, not your average Daymoor widow, different, definitely a higher-class type.

"Let's not have another scene," she said when I went over to see her. "Give me your hand on it."

So I gave her my hand and she held on to it for a minute and then she let go. I don't know how she managed it but when she took her own hand away I had a topaz ring in my hand. I tried giving it back to her. "Keep it," I said. "It's your engagement ring. You should hold on to it. It's yours. I gave it to you."

"I'm no longer engaged to be married," she said. "The wedding is canceled."

That was news to me. "What are you talking about?" I said.

"You know damn well what I'm talking about," she said. "And why."

"Hold on," I told her. "It takes two to make an engagement and it takes two to break it. I'm not breaking it."

"In this case," she said, "it took three."

"You mean you, me, and your son Roy?" I really got mad.

"No," she said. "I mean you, me, and your cleaning woman."

"You're not right about that," I said. "You've got it all wrong."

"Then sue me for breach of promise," she said. "It's over." I tried handing her back the ring but she wouldn't take it. "I couldn't wear that ring without feeling bad," she said. "Every time I'd put it on, I'd have to think about what might have been."

"It still can be," I said. "We can still get married."

"I already canceled the caterer," she said. She smiled at me. "I already canceled the florist. I already had notices sent out canceling the invitations."

I put the ring into my pocket. "At least you could have talked to me about it first," I said. "At least we could have talked things over."

She smiled at me again. If we ever did get married, I could end up hating that smile. "Talk what over? You must be kidding," she said. She was still smiling. "The bride's side pays for the wedding. I was paying the bills, so I did the canceling. All you have to cancel is the honeymoon."

I always had the feeling that she never wanted to go to New Orleans for the honeymoon anyway. The French Quarter isn't Paris, but it's good enough for me.

"Give the ring to your daughter-in-law," she said. "She likes it. I know that for a fact."

Let's not have another scene. Her words exactly. Who ever heard of breaking an engagement without a scene? She didn't even cry. That proves she's an old lady, as if I needed any more proof. She sure seemed old when she

said, "Let's not have another scene." Her face looked all
twisted and dried up. But I want to be a gentleman about
it. I'm not going to be caught saying even one word
against her. Nothing. Not a word. If that's the way she
wants it, separate, then so be it. That's the way she's going
to have it. Maybe her son Roy will fly down and take her
out to dinner every once in a while. She'll have to do
without my company. So be it.

Let's not have another scene. She said that and then she
hit me with the kicker, right in the balls: "You weren't ever
really in love with me anyway," she said. "You don't really
know what love means." What the hell was I going to do,
drag her over to the sack to show her that I know all there
is to know about love? Or try to force her to take back the
ring? Damned if later I didn't take that ring out of my
pocket and set it on the bathroom sink with my change
and my keys, and when I looked at it, it was exactly the
same color as the Listerine mouthwash I had sitting there.
It looked as if it came right out of the bottle. Maybe that's
why she never liked it. But she'd still be wearing it if she
hadn't been so nosy, poking around to spot Concepción
coming out of my door.

I don't really know what love means. That's what
she said. I was never really in love with her anyway. She
doesn't know what the hell she's talking about. I think
you're somebody who's incapable of love. It didn't seem
right to say, I already showed you just how capable I am.

That's what I was showing you all those nights in bed —
and you loved it. But no. Saying that would be making a
scene. Fuck her. Me, not capable of love. Me!

In love — what the hell does that mean anyway? God
knows, I was always plenty considerate, making sure I
took care of what she was feeling, in bed and outside of
bed too. That's what making love to a woman is, isn't it?
Making sure she gets to have as good a time as you're having, right? That's all anybody can ask, right: That's all,
right?

Isn't it?

I'M LUCKY in a way, I suppose, because he's not really a
well man, although I have to tell you, you can't see that
just from looking at him. But why else would he have
such a hard time catching his breath after just a little exercise? I hadn't seen him since we decided it's all over, no
wedding, we don't have a future; and then yesterday —
the very same day I'd picked out for the wedding, as it
happens — I bumped into him in the drugstore. He was
looking at the paperback book rack and I came around
the corner and practically walked right into him. I had to
go there for shampoo. Shampoo isn't what it used to be
for me. Maybe my hair is getting older and stiffer, breaking ends, all that business. I wanted to try this new kind

somebody told me about, Blond Always. They advertise it on TV shows. And there he was. When I spotted him I said "Oops." Just like that, "Oops." When I did that, he laughed, and he bowed down low and swooped his arm in front of himself as if he was saying, "Go straight ahead. Pass this way," and then he said "Madame." Maybe that was supposed to be a joke about our honeymoon in Paris or in New Orleans, but he got me smiling, and there I was giggling, just as if I was all ready to start up with him again. He is cute, and he knows it. And he was smiling at me, with the tip of his tongue touching his upper lip the way he does that, sort of flirting like, and it looked as if he was getting ready to start up with me all over again too.

In lots of ways he's been more fun than Monroe. He makes me feel like a kid. We certainly have a good time together. I have to admit it: I don't mind having a good time. But you can't go back to what's gone.

I don't know why that should be, but it's what everybody says.

But then why should I care what everybody says? I should be more concerned with what I want myself. Why shouldn't I have a visit with him again from time to time? Why shouldn't I enjoy myself? These days you don't have to get married to enjoy yourself. Nobody cares what we do. Who's watching? What have I got to lose? Maybe I ought to ask him over for dinner and take my chances on whether he'll come or not. Why shouldn't I? So long as he

keeps away from his bimbos, why shouldn't we get together again? Who's going to stop us?

We don't have to get married. We can be dear friends.
"Dear friend of." That's what it says all the time in the
death notices. "Formerly married to the late whatever the
wife's name was" — in this case it would be Alice — and
then they add "Dear friend of." That's where they'd put
my name. "Dear friend of Joyce Tarlow." That's what it
would say. Nobody I know would ever see it anyway because it would be in the Boston papers. It wouldn't even
be in *The Times*.

Anyway, he's not the only fish in the sea. As soon as
the news of our breakup got out and around, somebody called me up and asked me out to dinner. "Now
that you're available," he said. "Now that you're free." Of
course I said yes. Thank you, I'd love to. Yes. But I'm making him wait a week before I go out with him. Al Spear,
the nice-looking fellow who kept asking me to dance at
the installation.

So be it!
I walked out of there without even giving her a kiss
good-bye. That's the way the world ends, as the saying
goes, not with a bang but a whimper. Our banging days
are over, but she's not going to get me to go whimpering

after her. All I have to do is hang around the pool solo and the invitations will start coming in, especially when they know they won't have to invite her along too.

The day I bumped into her in the drugstore, it looked like she was getting herself available to start up all over again, but as far as I'm concerned, forget it. She had her chance. It looked like she was going to invite me over to her place for dinner again, but I didn't give her enough room to hand out the invitation. If I want to have dinner with an old lady, I can always get in touch with Rose. "Let me know if you're feeling hungry for a home-cooked meal sometime," Rose said to me down at the pool one day, "and I'll cook for you. I have to go into the hospital for a little bit next week, but let's make a date for when I come out."

Because she's going into the hospital, I felt I had to accept. "Sure," I told her. "Let's do it."

"I'll take my bottle of champagne out of the closet and put it on ice. It's got your name on it," she said. "It's dedicated to you."

But I don't need her either. I got younger ones to invite me over. There's this divorcée, Barbara. She even comes from Boston. Beautifully stacked. I happened to meet her coming out of the Activities Building, and she looked ready for a lot of activity. She looked eager for it, and activity's what I need. After the dry spell I've been through, courtesy of old lady Joyce, I deserve a bit.

Aʟ ꜱᴘᴇᴀʀ really knows how to show a woman a good time. He took me to Deary's, which is the finest restaurant around, and we had a wonderful time, lots of laughing. And he's really a gentleman. I told him I certainly hoped to be as friendly as he wanted but I was a woman who needed lots of courting, and he responded beautifully. Next week we are going to eat — I should say dine — at Exeter. He knows the right places, and he enjoys going to them. "In New York," he told me, "I used to eat in all the best places. Brussels. The Four Seasons. I really used to enjoy it."

He's a man who made a good living, I could see that. He used to live in Scarsdale, which is not exactly a slum.

I ᴡᴇɴᴛ into the hospital to visit Rose. I asked a couple of the guys who hung around the pool if they wanted to come along. After all those years of watching her in the exercise classes, you'd think they'd show a little interest. No customers. "Too depressing," that's what one of them told me. Harvey. "Too sad."

So I drove down there by myself. Harvey was right. It was depressing. There she was lying in bed, not endgame yet, no tubes coming out of her. But it was bad. I could tell that just from looking at her.

"No kiss?" she said to me when I walked into the room. So I leaned over and kissed her on the cheek. Then she introduced me to her daughter. This time things were bad enough to have her get her family to come down to Florida. A nice-looking girl, the daughter, tall like Rose. Vicky is her name.

"They're waiting for you down at the pool, Rose," I said to her. But we both knew she wasn't going to be showing up there again for a while, if ever. "Tell them I'll be getting back soon, good as new," she said. Talking was hard for her. To tell the truth, she looked so bad that after five minutes I was itching to get out of there. "I don't want to tire you out," I told her, and then the daughter said, "I'm only going to let you stay a few minutes anyway."

So I gave her another kiss good-bye and that was it. Good-bye, Rose. At least I had a nice date waiting for me when I got home — Barbara, my divorcée from Boston. I've been keeping her busy night and day. Or maybe I should say she's been keeping me busy. My place or her place, it doesn't matter. Both of us ready to go at it, all the time. And young. I don't know if she's even out of her fifties yet.

[IV]

Rose Billy Joyce

GRUEN, ROSE, of Daymoor Village, FL, formerly of Teaneck, New Jersey, in her 76th year. Beloved wife of the late Jacob (Jack) Gruen. Dear mother of Victoria Givler, adored grandmother of two, sister of Ethel Speiser, also of Teaneck. Graveside services at Jerusalem Cemetery in Peapack, New Jersey, 11:00 A.M., Oct. 5.

SYMMES, WILLIAM (Billy), suddenly at age 74, of Daymoor Village, FL, formerly of Brighton, well-known bandleader in the Boston area for many years before his retirement to Florida. He leaves behind a son, Dr. Mark Symmes of Newton, and one grandson. Services at Weinman Funeral Chapel, Beacon St., Brookline, at 10:30 A.M., Mar. 22, followed by interment at Sharon's Memorial Park. Memorial week at 279 Garland Road, Newton Centre.

SPEAR, JOYCE (Tarlow) in her 99th year at Palm Beach, FL, formerly of Daymoor Village, Florida, and before then of Flower Hill, Long Island, New York. Beloved mother of Robert Tarlow and Daniel Tarlow of New York City. Adored grandmother of eight, cherished great-grandmother of seven. Predeceased by her late husband, Monroe Tarlow, and her late second husband, Alfred Spear. Also predeceased by her beloved son Roy Tarlow. Services at Millman's Funeral Chapel, Northern Blvd., July 12 at 11:00 A.M.